consensually
COMPLICATED

BY NIAMH NORWOOD

First edition 2024

Cover art by Jade Pantin. Cover and interior design by Nathan Fréchette. Edited by Drew Gilvary, Shawn Brixi, and Deanna Broodhagen.
Legal deposit, Library and Archives Canada, May 2024.
Paperback ISBN: 9781990086687
Ebook ISBN: 9781990086755

Renaissance Press - pressesrenaissancepress.ca

Renaissance acknowledges that it is hosted on the traditional, unceded land of the Anishinabek, the Kanien'kehá:ka, and the Omàmìwininìwag. We acknowledge the privileges and comforts that colonialism has granted us and vow to use this privilege to disrupt colonialism by lifting up the voices of marginalized humans who continue to suffer the ongoing effects of ongoing colonialism.

Printed in Gatineau by
Imprimerie Gauvin - Depuis 1892
gauvin.ca
We acknowledge the support of the Canada Council for the Arts.

chapter
ONE

I was in love with falling in love. I've always been like that. I fall in love with couples in romance films. I fall in love with friends. I fall in love with everyone. I fall in love in an instant, and I fall hard. I give it my all each time. The feeling of being infatuated—when you've first met and the chemistry is developing—those are the times I feel *alive*. When I fall in love, I feel like I can do anything, *be* anyone. I feel elated to be seen as worth something for once in someone's eyes. To know that, for a few moments, I was the brilliant object of their affection. That makes it all worth it, all the struggling and competing for their love.

But I wasn't good at keeping relationships going. My relationships never lasted longer than a few months, but I would pursue those relationships with everything I had. It kept life interesting. I had trouble keeping a partner around for long. Once I moved past the infatuation, relationships often ended.

When I wasn't chasing new love, I painted. I usually worked with oil paints, and I had a decent following online. It was decent enough that I could make a living from my art. I loved the challenge it brought to my life. Every time I gained new followers, I'd get a hit of dopamine. And if I could accept the challenge by expressing myself through art, then why not do it?

I spent the last month isolated, barely speaking to anyone. I recently started a painting I called "Gen." It was for my most recent lost love. It was part of a series of sorts. I made a sketch or a painting every time I fell in love. Not just infatuation, but real love. If I painted someone every time I was infatuated, I'd have well over a hundred paintings crowding my apartment. I reserved that form of artistic expression solely for the people who truly touched me. The ones whose kisses lingered on my lips long after they left, that I thought of every day, and whose absence made me yearn for what was lost. It seemed odd, this yearning, when I always had someone new in my life—I would still miss my lost loves. People weren't replaceable, and neither were feelings.

I painted Gen and I sitting together, legs entwined, laughing. It was the moment we had first told each other that we loved one another. It had been months ago, but the memory was still vivid.

Gen had invited me over for dinner. It took me a while to drive to her place just outside of Kingston, but it was worth it. She had insisted on cooking one of my favourite dishes: creamy linguine with chicken. She had always been an excellent cook. After we ate, Gen opened a bottle of wine.

Gen was blonde and kept her hair naturally wavy. She wore simple gold dangling earrings and a little ring on her pinky finger. Her style was minimalist, but it worked for her.

"Here's to us," she said, pouring me a glass of wine.

"To us," I replied.

"You are the most amazing woman I've met in years, Bells..."

"Gen!" I exclaimed. "I'm really not."

"You are," she said, setting the wine bottle down on the counter. "I think so. And it's time you recognized it."

I had noticed the way Gen always looked at me. She looked at me like it might be the last time she ever saw me; like she wanted to memorize my features.

She was looking at me that same way at that moment from across the table.

I was thankful for the opportunity to talk. Gen was shy. It took time for her to openly express her feelings to me. I knew she wanted to be a better communicator. Her anxiety just seemed to get the best of her.

"I've been looking forward to this night for days," she said with a dazzling smile.

"I'm simply the bearer of good wine," I said, lifting my glass.

"Which show would you like to watch tonight?" Gen asked.

"I was thinking we'd finish *Gentleman Jack*. It's been so good. Like the lesbian *Pride and Prejudice* I never knew I needed."

"Yes. Let's do that." She motioned to my plate. "Did you like the linguine?" Her expression was so open and so vulnerable.

"I loved it," I said, and meant it. The fact that she had put that much effort in for me was flattering.

"Good," she said. "I was worried it wouldn't be as good as your favourite restaurant makes it."

"This is a thousand times better than my favourite restaurant!" I exclaimed, gesturing to the plate. "Because you made it for me. That means a lot."

I was struck in that moment by a desire to kiss her. I shot up from my chair and did just that. She melted into the kiss the way that only she ever did: her entire body relaxing, a smile spreading across her lips, and her hands running through my hair. When I pulled back, her eyes were half-lidded, and she looked at me dreamily.

"Wanna go to the living room?" she asked.

"The dishes…" I began, but she interrupted me.

"Forget the dishes. I just want to be near you."

I smiled. Though she was shy, she was direct when she wanted something.

"Okay, living room it is," I said.

We left our dishes on the table but brought our glasses and the remaining wine. I had already drained two glasses. The red on Gen's cheeks still hadn't faded, which meant she was probably feeling it too. When I looked at her, she seemed focused on her thoughts.

We turned on *Gentleman Jack* and held hands. She kissed my cheek. I felt so content, so at ease, that I kissed her back. She smoothed back my hair.

"You really are something, too, you know," I said.

"What does that mean?" she asked.

"It means you impress me," I replied. "You're so talented and charming. And yet you choose to spend your time with me."

She frowned. "I dance. How does that compare to all your great paintings?"

I kissed her again softly. "It's not a competition."

"I know," she whispered. "But you make me want to be better. For you."

"You're already everything I need," I said, and a realization occurred to me then, looking at her beautiful face with her flushed cheeks and hair in disarray. "I love you, Gen."

I suppose I had known before; I wouldn't have spent so much time trying to sketch her if I hadn't already known. Her eyes opened wide, and her lips parted slightly. "Really? You do?" She beamed. "That's great because I love you, too!"

I made a sound of delight and threw myself on her. She laughed, and we kissed. We lay there for what felt like hours before her roommate emerged from his room and banished us from the living room for being too noisy. I didn't mind. It meant we had to move to her bedroom instead.

A month had passed since then. Now I was back in my apartment, sitting on the floor, struggling with her smile.

I had printed out my favourite photos of her for reference. One was of us sitting next to a river on a sunny day, our faces pressed closely together. Another depicted our visit to an art gallery. That one was just of her, smiling next to her favourite find of the day, *Water Lilies* by Monet. There was one from when we went out for *taiyaki* and there was a bit of chocolate on my mouth. I remembered she had told me right after I took the picture and kissed me.

My favourite photo was from a series of portraits I had done of her in her apartment. She had turned to look at me from over her shoulder in the photo, the natural light from the window brightening her warm eyes. The eyes of someone in love. The picture might not have been a masterpiece, but I was glad to have caught it. That moment. Because I had lost it forever.

That's the thing about me: I fall in love fast, I fall in love often, but I do not fall out of love quickly. It turns to venom and pulses through my veins every moment of the day. Their absence and their rejection. Painting seemed to be the only way to excise them from my blood.

But I couldn't get her smile right. The smile that I had thought was only reserved for me, followed by that laugh. That beautiful, contagious laugh. As it turned out, it hadn't been reserved for me. There was someone else she loved who wanted her all for himself. And just like that, I lost her. Just like that, our moment of pure joy, of feelings exchanged, meant nothing. Now she shared it all with someone else.

I didn't want to linger on the breakup, painful as it was. I wanted to linger a little longer in the moment when we were happy together. So I did. With every stroke of my brush, I relived it. "I love you," I'd whisper to the canvas. I remembered how it felt to hear those words from her and how alive I had felt. "I love you."

I was extra careful painting her hair. It was one of my favourite things about her, and I wanted to get it exactly right. I placed a few strands behind her ears. That's how she always had it: tied up with a few loose strands behind her ears. I painted us holding hands and smiling, gazing into each other's eyes. That's how it had been. The way it was meant to be. Before Nate showed up and ruined it all.

I felt tears spring to my eyes, but I closed them shut tight until all I could think of was Gen in that pale blue dress reaching out for me. That was all I wanted to think about as I started painting myself. I used a mirror to get a sense of what I would have looked like smiling at her. I wanted this painting to be as accurate as possible. I painted my dark hair pushed away from my face. My skin was pale, so I mixed in some white paint to get the tone exactly right. My face looked a bit harsher than usual— it had lost much of its softness after the breakup. I hadn't been eating properly. There were shadows under my eyes that I left out of the painting. This was a painting of a happier time when those shadows didn't exist.

After a few hours of work—and a few glasses of wine—I had the start of something I was happy with. Normally, I wouldn't drink as much while I painted. I had a chronic history of migraines and I didn't usually want to make it worse by risking a hangover. However, tonight was an exception.

I had made her hair a bit more golden than it truly was. She looked radiant. That's how she had seemed to me at that moment. I washed my hands and changed my clothes. The next part would have to wait until later. I needed a break. My cat, Ghost, was sitting perched on the kitchen counter. Ghost was the white cat that Gen and I had rescued together from the shelter while we were dating. I pet Ghost's soft fur, and she purred. She blinked at me slowly. It had been difficult to spend the last month alone, but at least I had Ghost to keep me company.

I checked my phone sitting on the kitchen counter. There were eight messages, most from my best friend Alex. There was also one from Gen. "I miss you," was all it said. It stung to read that. There was also a message from the guy I had been seeing, Mark. It included a picture of him with a gaming controller in his hand. "Feel like playing?" read the attached text. I smirked. I may have spent the last few hours wallowing over a lost love, but Mark knew how to cheer me up. Cuddles and video games were among the keys to my heart.

Mark and I had met a few months ago but only started seeing each other when Gen and I broke up. He was the perfect mix of hot and geeky. Honestly, he had seemed too good to be true. The perfect rebound after my failed relationship with Gen. He was caring. Fun without being too relaxed. He knew when to be serious and when to be silly. And I was infatuated with him which relieved the sting of Gen a little bit. I had only been seeing him for a few weeks, but I already felt comfortable with him.

Mark was a digital artist, focusing on concept art at work. In his free time, he liked to draw video game and anime characters. He was well-known in his scene. We had spoken at the same conventions since meeting, and he was the one who had told their organizers about me for the event. We didn't paint the same kinds of things—he was more focused on video game art, whereas I painted original pieces. However, he had taken inspiration from my paintings when working on his video game. So, when the time came, he put in a good word for me. I appreciated his help.

But even his texts weren't enough to free my mind from my recent rejection. Only painting could do that. I poured myself another glass of wine and went back to the canvas.

It didn't take long before the bottle was finished and I was drunk. I checked my phone again. Gen's unanswered message sat in my inbox. I was almost insulted that she thought she could get back in my good graces by texting me. I thought about replying and telling her off, but I resisted. I didn't need any drama on top of my sadness.

But then, my phone dinged. It was a text from her.

> Gen: Hey Isabelle. I don't expect you to reply. But I want you to know that I'm sorry.

I needed to respond.

> Me: Sorry for what?
> Gen: I'm sorry for the way things ended between us.
> Me: Me, too.

I wanted to write more but deleted it. I didn't need to show her how broken I still was about it all.

> Gen: I was scared. That's why I ended things. I went with Nate because he was the easier choice.
> Me: Easier choice? What does that mean?

I was beginning to feel that this was the kind of conversation we should be having face-to-face.

> Gen: Easier than facing our issues.
> Me: Isn't this a conversation we should be having in person?
> Gen: I didn't think you'd want to meet up in person, given how you feel about me.

That pissed me off.

Me: Why would you assume you know how I feel?

Gen: I know how much I hurt you. I figured you'd hate me.

Me: I don't hate you, Gen. I'm hurt. There's a difference.

Gen: I really regret hurting you. So much.

I paused and stared at my screen. She seemed pretty genuine. But it was difficult to tell.

Me: If you want to continue this conversation, I'd rather we do it in person.

I thought she would ghost after that, but her response was immediate.

Gen: When works best for you?

Me: My schedule is pretty open.

Gen: How about right now? Are you free?

My chest tightened. I felt like I was choking. Now? I looked to the canvas still sitting out in the open in my apartment. I couldn't have her come here.

Me: I'm not free tonight. Maybe tomorrow morning?

Gen: All right. Let's do that.

I thought that was all, but then she added:

Gen: I look forward to it.

Was she sucking up to me? Why? Did she truly feel so guilty that she thought this was necessary? My chest tightened even further. Maybe this entire thing was a set-up so she could feel better about herself. She'd apologize, I'd tell her everything was fine, and she would continue living her happy new life with her new boyfriend.

But I'd give her the benefit of the doubt. If not for her, then at least for closure.

I texted Mark.

Me: I'll be coming over tonight. Sound good?

Mark: Sure. What's the special occasion?

Oh, I just need to see you because my ex texted me and now I'm stressed out to Hell and back.

Me: Nothing. Just wanted some company. See you in a few hours?

Mark: See you then :)

Mark and I didn't go out very often. Admittedly, that was probably because we spent most of our time in bed. It wasn't like we were dating, so there was no real reason to leave the house. We didn't go out to events. We only ever went out together to get food.

His room had become a familiar and comforting space to me recently. It was one of the few places where I didn't think about my breakup. I reserved all that angsty energy for when I was painting. When I was with Mark, I was blissfully happy. But something was missing. Even as I held him in my arms in bed, I felt like there was a distance between us.

"Hey," he said, inches away from my face. His brown hair was messed up, but it looked purposeful. He had put on a baggy gaming shirt and a pair of jeans. His brown eyes were wide. There was a hint of a smile on his lips.

"Hey," I replied.

"What are you thinking about?" he asked.

"What do you mean?"

"I can tell when you're thinking about something."

"How?"

"You bite your lip," he said, demonstrating. "Like that."

I immediately stopped biting my lip. "Sorry. I guess I've got a lot on my mind."

"Does it have to do with... what happened?"

I didn't know exactly what he meant, but I could guess. It was either about my depressive episode or my breakup with Gen—or both. The nice thing about Mark was that I could confide in him. He was completely open to hearing my feelings for other people. I wished he was a little more romantic, but I enjoyed his companionship.

"Yeah," I said. "I'm still a little broken up about it."

"But you're painting again, right?" he asked, then kissed my cheek. "I assume that's why you've been leaving me on read so often."

"I don't mean to leave you on read," I said quickly. "It's just that when I'm working, I get really focused..."

"You don't have to explain yourself," he said kindly. "I'm an artist too, remember? I know how it is when you're in the zone."

I relaxed. "Thanks for understanding."

"Although it does hurt a bit when I send you a picture of myself and you don't even respond," he teased. Did I detect a hint of disappointment in his voice?

"Maybe I'm too in awe of how great you look."

He laughed. "All right, all right. Flattery will only get you so far."

"I think I've gotten pretty far," I said, trailing a finger up his chest.

He shoved a pillow in my face. "Mess off."

I moved the pillow out of the way. "You love it."

Thankfully, he was smiling. "I do enjoy my time with you, yes."

"I enjoy it too."

The truth was, I probably enjoyed it too much. I loved the feeling of his arms wrapped around me. It felt so comforting. And when I breathed in, I could smell him. There was always a hint of sandalwood-scented cologne on him. There were times I had dreamt about cuddling with him and woke up disappointed when he wasn't there. I hadn't shared any of this with him.

"What else is on your mind?" he asked, stretching.

I admired his arms as he stretched. "You, to be honest."

"What about me?" he asked.

"Mostly how gorgeous you are." I kissed him. He kissed me back. It felt so natural. I pulled away. "But you already know that."

"I don't mind hearing it more than once," he said. The warmth in his eyes sent shivers down my spine. But brief flirtations here and there would never be enough to satisfy me.

"The truth is, I've been finding it difficult being alone most of the time."

"You're not completely alone," he said, taking my hand. "I know I'm not a partner, but I'm still here for you."

"I know," I said, feeling guilty. Even though he was there for me, it wasn't exactly the way I wanted. "But I've been missing the thrill. Getting close to someone emotionally. When I don't have it in my life, things seem boring."

"Boring?" he asked, arching a brow. "Is what we did really boring to you?"

"Well, no, that's not what I meant—"

He laughed. "I know, I know. Don't worry. I'm just teasing you. I understand why you'd feel that way. You weren't the one who ended things, after all. It can be hard when you're the one being dumped."

"Yeah."

"It might be good for you to get out there again. Try to meet new people."

I thought about my painting of Gen. Now that I had painted my feelings of regret about the breakup, was I finally ready to move on?

"You're right," I said slowly.

I wasn't thrilled that Mark was telling me to meet other people, but I knew that was the realistic approach. I needed to move on from him and Gen, and perhaps he was gently pushing me in that direction because he knew how I felt about him. I paused. That line of thinking wouldn't get me anywhere positive. I had no idea how he felt about me because I hadn't had the courage to express my own feelings.

I wanted to go home. I knew it wasn't entirely healthy to want to self-isolate as much as I did, but...

"I should get going," I said.

"I figured you'd want to go home and work," he replied. "You've got that look in your eye."

I slid off his bed and retrieved my clothes. "You sure are observant."

"If you say so." He wrapped his arms around my waist. "If you're ever feeling down, you can talk to me. You know that, right?"

I kissed him quickly. "I know that. Thank you."

"Good." He released me and stepped back. "I hope painting goes well tonight."

"Thanks," I replied. "Me, too."

When I got home, I lay on my bed with a happy sigh. Ghost curled up on my chest and purred, and I gave her a few pets. My time spent with Mark gave me the morale boost I needed. Though I had to admit there were now bittersweet feelings attached to him, I liked him. Probably more than I should.

I had told him that I was going to do some more painting tonight, but my only intention was to crawl into bed and try to forget about my ex. I spent the rest of the night with my earbuds in, trying to relax while listening to soothing music. I'd need to be relaxed for the meeting with Gen in the morning.

Chapter
TWO

My first date with Gen had been over tea. Our connection was what made it wonderful. I loved her look as soon as I laid eyes on her. Even without makeup, she was radiant. I remember walking into the tea shop and feeling shocked by her beauty. I remember being happy she was interested in me.

And then, of course, she wasn't interested in me. Walking into the tea shop now, I was hit by a wave of nausea and nostalgia. She was sitting in our usual spot wearing a loose white dress. Seeing her stabbed at my heart. It seemed a little cruel to pick the spot we had spent so many hours holding hands and reminiscing over old memories. But, despite not loving her choice of seating, I sat down next to her.

"Hi," I said shortly. I had barely been sitting for ten seconds, and I was already choked up. Seeing people after a breakup was always hard, especially when they were probably only seeing you to get forgiveness.

"Hi," she replied. Her voice wavered.

I wondered if it was as difficult for her as it was for me. "It's kind of hard for me to be here again with you," I confessed.

"I worried that it might be," she said. "I'm sorry."

"Then why did you suggest we come here?" I asked.

"Because I thought it might bring back good memories," she said. "That's what I had hoped, anyway."

I sighed in frustration. "Gen, the only good memories we have here are from when we were together. Coming here once we're broken up changes things a bit, don't you think?"

She wrung her dress in her hands. "True. I was just hoping that..."

She didn't finish her sentence.

"That what?" I asked.

"That you might forgive me."

There it was. The line I had been expecting all along. That was why she had contacted me: because she didn't want to feel responsible for hurting my feelings anymore. She wanted to make it all go away with the magic words: "I'm sorry."

I didn't expect her to cry.

"When things with Nate didn't work out, I realized how stupid I had been..." she continued.

I paused. "Things didn't work out with Nate?"

She shook her head. "No. We only lasted two weeks."

"I'm sorry that happened," I said.

"No, you're not," she said. "I know how angry you were when Nate and I got together."

"Because I thought what happened between us was real."

"It *was* real!" she exclaimed, turning a few heads from the tables around us. She lowered her voice. "I was the one who made a mistake."

"You're saying that leaving me was a mistake?" I asked. I noticed how close she was to me. She inched her hands closer to my leg.

"It was a complete mistake." She blinked away her tears. "Can you forgive me?"

"What are you asking?" My heart vaulted against my chest. "If you want my forgiveness, then fine, you have it. But if you're telling me that you regret what you did…"

"I do."

"What do you expect me to say?" I asked. "It took you a month to figure out that you missed me. I've been crying every night missing you! I even…" I stopped myself, but she noticed.

"Even what?"

"I even painted you," I admitted.

"I'd like to see it sometime," she said as if I invited her to my place.

I'm sure it must have been evident to her by the look of hope on my face that I wanted her back. But fear of being hurt again kept me from acting on it.

"If you regret leaving me, then why are you here?" I asked. "To see if I want to get back together?"

"I want you back," she said. "But I needed the time apart to figure that out."

"Why did you break up with me? Because I wasn't enough?" I asked.

"No!" she said. "That's not why at all. I told you, it's because I was too scared of facing our issues. Like how I wasn't there for you with your depression. The sleep talking was a lot for me, too. You know, when you'd wake up crying? But I've come to terms with it now. I don't want to lose you."

As if she hadn't already lost me. I pressed a hand to my forehead. "I don't know, Gen. I'm still so fragile from you leaving me for Nate. How would I ever be able to trust you again?"

"I want you back," she repeated. "But while we were apart, I realized something about myself."

I frowned. "Okay."

She looked at me pleadingly. "Please understand. It's entirely new to me, too. But while we were apart, I realized I'm polyamorous."

I froze. *Polyamorous*? That felt like a double-edged sword. I could have the woman I loved back, but I would have to share her. That's what she was offering me.

"So, you're saying that... if we got back together... we'd be seeing other people, too," I said slowly.

I wondered if that was something I could do. Would I be able to handle Gen going out on dates with other people after everything that had happened between us? Would I be comfortable seeing Mark, knowing Gen was out there waiting to hear from me?

She nodded. "I think so, yes. That seems to be what's right for me."

"Is that why you broke up with me? Because I wasn't enough?" I asked. I couldn't handle how many times my hopes had been dashed in a single evening.

"No!" she said. "That's not why at all. But now that I've come to terms with the fact that I'm polyamorous, I've also come to terms with the fact that I don't want to lose you."

I considered what she was offering. I had never dated polyamorously before in my life. I had no way of knowing if it would even work for me. If Gen and I got back together, and she was dating other people, I wouldn't have to stop seeing Mark. I could continue to date both people I like. I saw some advantages to this, but my heart still ached at the thought of getting back together.

I pressed a hand to my forehead. "I don't know, Gen. I'm still so hurt from you leaving me for Nate. How would I ever be comfortable being with you while you dated someone else?"

She took my hand from my forehead and held it. "Right now, the only person I'm interested in dating is you. I just need you to know that, in the future, I might be interested in other people too."

"When?" I asked. I liked the feeling of her hand touching mine way too much. I withdrew my hand. "I don't know if I could date you knowing that our exclusivity has a deadline."

"Don't think of it as a deadline," she said. "Think of it as me taking time to focus on you and heal our relationship. Whatever happens next happens."

I deeply wanted to heal our relationship. I did. I wanted to fix things between us more than anything. The way she made me feel while we were laying on that couch together, when she had told me she loved me, was beautiful. I wanted more of that feeling. But knowing that she was polyamorous now didn't help things at all.

"How do you know you're really polyamorous?" I asked. "I mean, you've never really lived that lifestyle before, have you?"

"I realized when I was with Nate that I could have feelings for more than one person at a time," she said. "I realized that because of you. Because I still loved you so much, despite being with him. That's when I knew that one person could never satisfy me because I wanted all kinds of experiences."

"Or maybe Nate and I just weren't the right people for you," I said. I felt a sinking sensation in my stomach.

"No! I know how I feel about you. I've never been more certain of anything in my life." She looked up at me with pleading eyes. "I *love* you."

"I feel dizzy," I announced. "This is just a lot to take in at once."

"I know, and I'm sorry."

"The woman I love leaves me after telling me she loves me. Then she comes back a month later saying she wants me back but that I'd have to share her." I shook my head. "I feel like I'm going to explode."

"What if we just dated until we felt comfortable with each other and addressed the poly thing later?" Gen asked.

"No," I said immediately. "I can't just pretend we're monogamous for like six months only to switch things up after that. Whatever we choose to do, we'd have to do it from the start."

"Then we'd be open from the start," Gen said. "Is that something you think you could do?"

I paused and looked down at my lap.

"What are you thinking?" she asked softly.

"I'm thinking of how I felt when you left me for Nate," I replied. "It hurts like hell. So, thinking of you with other people..."

"Except it wouldn't be like it was with Nate," she said. "I know I hurt you with him. Broke your trust. I won't do that again. With other people, it would be different. You would know everything about them. And you would also know that I wouldn't leave you for them."

"I know it might be different." I met her gaze. "But I'm not certain I can do that after what I went through with our breakup."

"I'm sorry," she said. Gen pressed her lips together. She was wearing lip gloss. I wished I could taste it again, but I also knew that moving too fast right now could be perilous. "But I needed all of that to happen to figure out what I really wanted."

"And you're saying that *part* of what you want is me," I said. I frowned. "It's not as romantic when I put it like that. The fact that I'm only part of what you want. That I'm not special."

"That's not true," she retorted. "You *are* special to me. It's just that I don't think I could ever just be with one person."

"Doesn't that kind of ruin the romance of it all?" I asked.

"I don't think so." Gen leaned in, ran her fingers through my hair, and kissed me. I melted under her touch and leaned into her, smelling her body lotion. She smelled so good, just like I remembered. Her lip gloss tasted like vanilla. When she pulled back, her eyes were twinkling. "Did that not feel romantic?"

My breathing was shaky. "It did."

"Then the romance between us isn't ruined."

"Kissing isn't all there is to romance," I said. "I like to feel special."

"And didn't I make you feel special?" Gen asked. "Before?"

"Well, yes..." I spoke hesitantly.

"Then I can make you feel special again," she said. "If you give me another chance."

"Is it really special if you're sharing, though?" I asked.

I wanted to fix things between us more than anything. The way she had made me feel was beautiful. I wanted more of that feeling. But, with her, it came with a cost. One that was too high for me.

"What are you thinking?" she asked softly.

I met her gaze. "I don't think I can see you again."

"It'll be different this time," she said.

"I don't think so. And even if it was different this time, I don't want to risk getting hurt like that again."

"I wish I could go back and change everything," Gen said.

She leaned in and ran her fingers through my hair.

I stopped her. "I can't."

She looked disappointed. "Did that not feel romantic?"

"It felt like heartbreak," I said. "It doesn't feel right anymore."

"Didn't it feel right before?" Gen asked.

"Well, yes..."

The way Gen made me feel was beyond anything anyone else made me feel. My instincts were telling me to take her into my arms and not let her go. But, then again, I could've been confusing my instincts with my fear of being alone.

"You have a lot to think about, I know," she said. "I didn't expect you to have an answer for me right away."

"I don't know what to feel, Gen," I said. "Give me time to think about it, okay?"

"Okay. I will."

I cleared my throat. "Can I ask how you've been?"

"I've been okay, but you've been on my mind a lot," she said.

"Me too," I replied.

"Why didn't you ever text?" Gen asked. "I'm a good listener."

It was too painful to think of her living a happy life with Nate. And that's what I would have thought about each time I talked to her.

"I didn't want to bother you," I lied.

"You wouldn't have bothered me," she replied. "I would have liked to have heard from you."

"Well, you're hearing from me now, at least."

She smiled. Everything about her smile warmed me, even after all the betrayal. "I'm glad for that."

"Gen?"

"Yeah?"

"I think I can forgive you," I said. "For all the Nate stuff. But it'll take time to earn back my trust."

"I'll respect whatever you choose." She paused. "Although I'm curious. Is there someone else in your life?"

I frowned. "It might be a bit early to ask for details like that."

"You're right. I totally went too fast with that one. I don't mean to make you uncomfortable."

"It's all right," I said. "I have questions, too. Like, was dating Nate worth it?"

She winced. "No. It wasn't. But, like I said, it led me to knowing what I really want."

Somehow, that comforted me. It seemed Nate meant very little to her if she discarded him so easily. But, then again, she discarded *me* rather easily too. The breakup had been abrupt. And then she announced she found happiness elsewhere. It wasn't easy to come back from that.

"I think I need some time alone to reflect," I said.

"Of course," she replied. "Whatever you need."

We said our goodbyes outside the café. We hugged quickly.

When I got home, I pulled out the painting I had done of her on the couch with me, laughing with her hair streaming over her shoulders. It had been the last time we told each other, "I love you." I didn't want to destroy the painting despite the pain it brought. I had put so much time and feeling into it that I couldn't just get rid of it. I hid it from view. If it was hidden, I could focus on the present instead of the past.

I needed advice on what to do about Gen, and the only person I could think to ask was Mark. I didn't want to bother my other friends with more questions about my ex. They would likely tell me to move on because Gen had been deceitful.

What I didn't expect was for Mark to have that exact same advice.

"She's using your feelings for her to get what she wants," he said.

Miraculously, I had convinced Mark to meet me outside of his apartment. We were out for ramen. The salty soup and the thick noodles warmed me and eased my anxiety. I slurped from my spoon in frustration.

"Why would you say that? I don't think she's using my feelings at all."

"She knows you love her, right?"

"Yes."

"Then she has leverage. You're blinded by love."

"She's giving me time to think about it," I said. "Sorry. I know I sound a little defensive."

"Yes, but what's the alternative? Did she ever tell you that? What happens if you don't want to be polyamorous? Will she just throw you away again?"

I hadn't considered that. What *would* she do if I told her I couldn't be polyamorous? Mark was asking some good questions.

"I don't know. I assume she'd be okay being friends."

"Did she tell you that?" he asked. "I know you want to be friends with her after all this passes. But she might not feel the same way. She might only want to date you. If she can't have that, she might not want anything to do with you at all."

"I hope that's not the case..."

"If you ask her, it should clear things up a bit. Then you'll know if she's giving you an ultimatum or an actual choice."

"True."

Mark slurped some noodles with his chopsticks. He wiped his mouth with a napkin. "Do you think you could actually be poly?"

"I think so, yes," I replied.

"Why? I've never heard you talk about it before," he said flatly.

"Because I've had feelings for multiple people at the same time before," I said.

"Really? When?" he asked. "Because when you're in love with someone, they're all you talk about. Day and night. When you're talking about love, I've never heard more than one person's name pass your lips at the same time."

I couldn't think of a clever or suave way to tell him that the second person I liked was him. But it was true; I was in love with Gen and infatuated with Mark. There were two people in my life I had feelings for, and Gen was offering me a relationship where I could have both. There wouldn't have to be any love triangles, and there wouldn't have to be any conflict. I could have both people I liked.

The problem was that Mark definitely did not like me back.

"I feel like a pathetic mess," I moaned, stretching my arms over the table.

"You are *not* a pathetic mess," he said, taking my hands.

I tried to stop from blushing, but it was hard when he touched me, especially in public. I retrieved my hands quickly. "Thank you. You're too kind. But I'm feeling pretty pathetic. I have the girl of my dreams offering to get back together, and here I am whining about it."

"I think it's perfectly valid to have some fears about it all," he said. "Even I had a bit of anxiety when I started dating non-monogamously."

"Really? Even you?" I asked incredulously.

"Yeah. It can be hard to deal with other people's emotions. Sometimes, even one person can be overwhelming. So, when you add several into the mix, it can become too much to handle," Mark explained.

"Were the women jealous, or...?"

"Yeah, jealousy was one problem," he said. "It was a lot of drama. That's when I decided I'd keep things easy and not get too involved."

"Right." I tried not to sound disappointed. "I'm worried about how jealousy would affect me with Gen. I already lost her once, and I'd be scared to lose her again."

"I hear you," he replied. "But you don't have to enter a relationship with her again if you don't want to. If polyamory sounds like your thing, then great! But, remember, it's not something you necessarily have to explore with her."

"But I love her," I said. "Surely it would be easier to do it with her than someone I've never met."

"I don't know," he said. "You might be surprised how well you can get along with a new person with similar interests."

I narrowed my eyes. "Did you have someone in mind?"

He lifted his hands into the air as a sign of peace. "I'll come clean. I was thinking of setting you up with one of my friends."

"And you wouldn't happen to be *dating* this friend, would you?" I asked.

"We dated briefly," he said. "But I think you'd really like each other. You have a lot in common besides me. You're both fierce and creative. I think you'd be a power couple."

"A power couple, huh?" I asked, lifting a brow. "I think you've been watching too many matchmaking shows on Netflix."

"I'm trying to make the top matchmakers proud."

"You're unbelievable."

"I try my best to be," he replied.

This conversation didn't faze me too much. Maybe it was because I trusted Mark. He was always mindful when we spoke. I felt like he actually listened to me. And now, as we discussed polyamory, I felt he cared about my well-being.

"What's her name?" I asked, giving in a little.

He beamed. "Narisha."

"That's a pretty name," I said. "What does she do?"

"She works as a teaching assistant at the university."

"Nice. So, she's smart, too."

"Yep. I imagine I've made a great match."

"Oh, and what makes you so sure?" I asked.

"I think I have good reason to be confident, actually," he said. "I don't know if you've noticed, but we've been spending lots of time together. I've gotten to know you pretty well."

I *had* noticed. "Okay, so you know me. Fine. That doesn't make you an expert matchmaker. And is she non-monogamous like you?"

"She is indeed," he said. "And she's in search of a partner. She complains that she can't find someone that meets all her standards."

"And you think that person is me."

"I didn't...until this conversation happened," he said. "Now I think you'd be perfect."

"Hold on." I pointed a chopstick at him. "What if things work out between this Narisha girl and me? What then? Do we both keep seeing you, too?"

He shrugged. "If that's what you want."

"It's way too early to tell. I haven't met her yet."

He leaned forward. "But you're interested?"

For a guy with no love life of his own, he seemed set on arranging things with others.

"I wouldn't mind learning more about her," I said.

He showed me his phone. "Here's her Instagram."

Her long brown hair was curled loosely in the photo. Her makeup was spot on. Her eyelashes were long and thick in the close-up photos. There were photos of her going on hikes. That would gain her points with my best friend, for sure. She wore the most gorgeous gold rings. Her outfits ranged from rompers to sweatpants and tank tops, but they all looked fashionable.

"Is she a photographer?" I asked. "She has some high-quality pics."

"Yeah," Mark replied. "She does photoshoots now and then and posts them to Instagram. You should follow her."

"Oh, I will," I said, and I must've sounded eager because he laughed.

"We need to get you a date."

"I thought that's what we were doing," I said, motioning to our table.

"Yes, but you need another." There was that confident smile again. "Luckily for you, I'm great at getting people together."

"Why does this excite you so much?" I asked. "I'd think after all the drama you experienced with your previous partners that you'd keep to yourself."

"This is different," he said. "Besides, I can always bow out when things get messy."

"Oh, so you plan for them to get messy?" I asked.

"No! I hope things don't get messy at all." He took a bite out of the pork from his bowl. "But I think you should seriously consider refusing Gen. I don't think anything good will come of that."

"Because I'd be getting back together with my ex?"

"Because she's hurt you once before, and I don't want to see you hurt like that again."

I both loved and hated the way he cared about me. I loved it because it meant he had some kind of feelings for me. But I hated it because I knew he didn't feel the same as I did.

"So, how did you meet her?" I asked. "If I'm going on a date with her, I have to at least know the details."

"Are you sure? I thought the fact she dated me was a turn-off for you."

"I can't fault her for that."

He laughed. "Fair enough. I met Narisha at a party."

"So, she likes to party," I said. "I don't really fit into that scene."

"It wasn't a rave," he said. "It was at a café. A little show put on by a local band. She was there supporting them."

"Oh, that sounds nice," I said. "What were you doing there?"

"I was bored, and it was across the street from my place," he said.

"So, you met at this concert and went home together?"

"Basically, yeah."

The strange thing was, I didn't feel jealous thinking of Mark dating her. I was glad that he had enjoyed his time with her. I wondered if I didn't feel jealous because I wasn't in love with Mark yet. Did a person only feel jealousy when they were in love? I couldn't ask him about it without revealing how I felt about him, so I let it go.

"Well, I'll add her on Instagram and see how it goes," I said. I went onto the app and pressed follow.

He smiled. "Nice!"

"God, you are like some kind of fanfic reader getting all excited over your 'ship.'"

"I need something to keep me occupied these days," he said simply.

I loved how easy it was to talk to him. I loved how funny he was and how at ease I felt when I was around him. And now, he was setting me up with a potentially good match. I was excited to see if she lived up to my expectations.

But I still didn't really know what to do about Gen. Mark had made himself clear. He thought Gen was bad news. And maybe she was. She had already broken my heart once—who was to say she wouldn't do it again? And the whole polyamory thing made things messy. I didn't even know if I could be polyamorous, and I certainly didn't want to experiment with someone I already *loved*. But maybe if I could try it out with someone new—someone I wasn't deeply attached to—maybe I could figure out if my personality was compatible with the lifestyle.

My phone chimed, and I checked it. It was a notification from Instagram. Narisha had followed me back.

Chapter
THREE

I had been putting off working on commissions because I had been so wrapped up in all the Gen drama and working on my painting of me and her. Now that her painting was out of the way, I could focus on the work that got me paid. I started by sketching a painting, drawing the lines of a woman's face and figure, and a rough sketch of the environment surrounding her.

My phone chimed. It was a text from my best friend, Alex.

Alex: Want to go for an easy hike after work?

Me: A hike? Why?

Alex: Why not?

Me: Because it requires activity. You know I don't like moving.

Alex: Come on, it'll be a nice break after working.

She was right—I had been crouching around my apartment all day. But that had left me sore and wanting a hot bath, not exercise.

Me: What's in it for me?

Alex: You get to spend time with your best friend in the world?

I rolled my eyes.

Me: Fine. What time works for you?
Alex: Let's say 4:00.

I had until then to get as much work as possible done on my painting. I finished sketching it and then proceeded to pick the colours. My client had requested it be mysterious, so I'd be using primarily dark colours. I put on my easy-listening playlist and got to work. I loved it when I was in the zone. It was as if nothing mattered except me, the paint, and the canvas.

Clients didn't require me to invent a backstory for every character I created, but I did. It was part of why I loved to paint. When I created someone, I came one step closer to understanding them. I wanted to understand people.

By 2:00, I had something I was proud of. It wasn't finished, but it was a great start. The colours had created movement on the still life of the sketch, and the final piece was taking shape. Ghost was stretched out before the canvas, meowing and demanding attention. I stepped away from my work and petted her before getting ready.

In the bathroom, I washed my face and straightened my hair. I didn't have to look especially good since we were going to exercise and would probably get sweaty anyway, but I still wanted to make an effort. I put on my black yoga pants and navy blue top, grabbed my purse, and went to meet Alex at the trail.

As soon as I walked to the trailhead, I regretted coming. I didn't really want to climb any steep hills. I spotted Alex farther in, who seemed ready to go. Her blonde hair bobbed on her short frame as I watched her stretch her legs wide from her body, holding herself up with her hands. Even from the entrance to the trail, I swear I could see her biceps and calves flex and bulge through her dark blue activewear. I considered making a break for it, but she saw me.

"Hey! Over here!" she exclaimed, waving me over. I had no choice but to join her.

"Hey," I said. "Your stretching looks... intense."

"Oh, don't worry about doing it, too," she said. "I just find it can help before a workout."

"That's what I was afraid of. A workout."

"It won't be too much for you, will it?" She frowned. "Maybe this was a bad idea."

"No! It's fine. I didn't move much today, so I still have some energy. I have enough left to do this. It's one of my good days, anyway. So, you don't have to worry."

"I'm glad to hear it, then." She slapped my shoulder playfully. "How've you been?"

"I've been all right," I said.

"Have you been getting out much?" she asked. Alex may as well have been the social police. She liked to check in every week to make sure I was socializing enough. It was sweet of her, but it could be a little overbearing.

"I've been getting out enough," I said.

"Still seeing Mark?" she asked.

"Yep," I said. "I went to him for advice recently."

"Advice on what?"

"Gen got in touch with me again," I told her.

Alex handed me a water bottle. "She what?"

"She texted me."

"And what did that jerk say?" Alex asked, her tone rising.

"Please don't call her that," I said quietly.

"She threw you aside for the first shiny new thing that came her way. How can you even think of defending her?" Alex had her hands on her hips. "What did she say?"

"She invited me out for tea."

"And you went?" Alex asked, mouth agape.

"Yes."

Alex's eyes were stormy. "I can't believe you went for tea with her."

"Apparently, she needed time to figure herself out." I took a shaky breath. "She said that she's polyamorous now."

"Oh, great for her," Alex said, rolling her eyes. She walked down the first path. I followed. "Now she can have her cake and eat it, too."

"What does that mean?" I asked. I was sweating already.

Alex slowed her pace. "It means now she can have everything she wants, no consequences."

"I don't think she's that shallow!"

"I do!" she replied. "She just puts on an act, and now she's got you fooled!"

I paused. Could that be true? Could it all have been an act just to get what she wanted? If both Alex and Mark thought she was manipulating me, maybe they were right. "It's possible I'm letting my emotions blind me on this," I admitted. "I just don't want that to be the case."

Alex hopped over a fallen branch in her way. "Look, I'd love for Gen to be a good person, too. But she's not. She'll just use you until she gets what she wants, and then she'll dump you again for the next new thing. Or maybe she'll decide that you're not suited for the polyamorous lifestyle."

"That's the thing," I said. "It might not matter. I have a date."

She nearly slipped. "Really?"

"Really," I confirmed. "I think I might be able to have feelings for more than one person at a time. I spoke with Mark about it. He's labelling himself as polyamorous now. I thought I would try it out, too."

"Oh, boy." She shook her head. "You have a lot to learn about non-monogamy."

"Then teach me," I said. "I'm a quick study."

"I know," she said. "You are just a little naïve, though."

"Well of course I am," I retorted. "This is the first time I've ever really had to think about it all. Before, I went with the flow, which was monogamy. Nobody ever offered me more than one option before."

Alex turned to face me. "That doesn't make you poly. Plenty of people have feelings for more than one person at once. Why do you think people cheat so much? But that doesn't make them polyamorous."

"But they could be if they did it ethically," I said.

"They don't want to do it ethically. Let me put it another way. There are plenty of monogamous people with crushes that they never act on. Because they're committed to someone. Do those crushes make them poly?"

"I think they could be if they wanted to," I said.

Alex sighed. "I don't know."

"It's true! If they have the potential to love more than one person at a time, then they can be poly. That's the whole premise, isn't it?"

"I've been in poly relationships before, and it's not all love all the time," she said.

"No relationship is."

"But polyamory brings its own drama."

"Okay," I said. "I believe you."

"Let's pick up the pace."

We quickened to a light jog. I struggled to keep up. Doing new things always made me anxious. That's the way I was, even if the new things were fun like this. I was always afraid of having a flare-up and not being able to do it as well as everyone else. In this case, I was terrified of slipping and falling on my face, too.

But I kept up the pace. I had rested enough in the last week that I had enough energy to do this. That's what I told myself, anyway. I was much slower than Alex, but that didn't stop me. Slow and steady, right?

"I agree with Mark," Alex said. "Gen's using your feelings against you to put you in a situation you don't want to be in."

"But that's the thing, I might not mind polyamory."

"Maybe not, but I doubt trying with Gen will bring back good memories. Like I said, she just wants to have her cake and eat it too."

I started to feel dizzy, but I pressed on. "You're right. Maybe she really does have ulterior motives."

"I think leaving Gen in the past is the best idea," Alex said. "There might be new people in your future. Better people."

I paused. "Oh. I don't feel so good."

"Want to slow down?" she asked, her tone shifting to concern. "Don't worry, I got you."

"Yes," I said, pressing my eyes tightly shut. We found a park bench nearby and sat down.

"A flare-up with your migraines?" she asked, looking remorseful.

"Yeah," I said. "Maybe I've been pushing myself too hard with work lately. I did start working on a personal project despite all my commissions. Probably not the best move."

"Let's go get a cup of tea to calm you down," she said. "That's the nice thing about hiking here. It has a tea shop nearby."

We walked for a few minutes outside of the trail before reaching the street. The tea shop was there. We found the seating area, and I covered my face with my hands to hide my eyes from the bright lights. They were making the headache worse. Alex returned to the table with two chai lattes and a couple of ibuprofen pills.

"Here, take this," she said.

I popped them in my mouth and took a swig of tea. "Hopefully, those will kick in soon," I said. "Thank you for helping me out."

"Of course," Alex said, taking a seat before me. "I'm sorry."

"What, why?"

"If I hadn't pushed you to come out, you wouldn't feel like crap right now," she said.

"That's not how it works," I replied. "I really thought I had rested enough recently, but I guess I haven't."

"You always think you've rested enough," she remarked.

"So, then, it's my fault, not yours," I said. "Don't blame yourself for asking me out to have fun. Unfortunately, my body had other things in mind."

"Like a migraine."

"Sadly." I ran a hand through my hair. "Sometimes I worry these health issues are going to get in the way of my love life, too."

"How so?" Alex asked.

"Gen was always so mad at me when I would get migraines. We'd be watching a movie or something, and then we'd have to turn it off because of me. Or when we'd go out for a hike or something but would have to turn around and come home after five minutes. She hated that."

"I don't think other people are going to be that unreasonable," Alex said. "I think most people who care about you will understand that it's beyond your control. Like I do. Not everyone thinks like Gen does." Her expression grew gentler. "So, what are you going to do about this poly stuff?"

"I think I'm going to try it out," I said. "Why not? It's the time for new beginnings and all of that, isn't it?"

"Yes, but new beginnings usually don't involve exes..."

"Not with Gen," I said. "I meant with someone else. A woman named Narisha. Mark knows her. He said he thinks we're a perfect match."

"Narisha..." Alex repeated. "I know that name. I've heard it before."

"Really?" I asked though I wasn't entirely surprised. The sapphic community was small. Everyone had dated everyone at this point. "How do you know her?"

"I think she dated Ashley," Alex said. She picked up her phone and apparently started scrolling Ashley's Instagram. "She's an Instagram friend of mine. I think she had a few old pictures up with Narisha."

I waited impatiently as she scrolled and scrolled. Could it be? Did Alex really have some background information on this person I was being set up with? And if she did, did I want to hear it before I even met her?

"Oh, here it is!" Alex exclaimed and turned the screen toward me. It was a photo of the woman I recognized as Narisha from her profile with another woman who was a bit shorter than her with brown hair and a cute smile.

"Wow," I said. "Small world."

"Totally." A smile spread across Alex's lips. "You know what this means, right?"

I narrowed my eyes. "No, what does it mean?"

"It means we can ask her questions about Narisha before your date!"

"Hold on a second," I said, lifting my hands into the air. "All I did was follow her on Instagram. How do you know she'll even say yes when I ask her out?"

"Because, knowing Mark, he's probably set it all up already without you even knowing," Alex said. I considered that notion. It was true: that was pretty on-brand for Mark. "If he's spoken to you about it, then he's already spoken to her, too."

"So, you want to spy on her by asking Ashley questions?" I asked.

"It's not spying. It's finding out what you're getting yourself into," Alex said. "A bit of investigation before a date is wise." I rolled my eyes as she opened the messenger app on her phone. "All right. I'm texting Ashley now."

"What?" I froze. "Alex, no! Do not text her!"

"Too late," she said, pleased with herself. "Already sent."

"What did you say?" I asked in horror.

"If she was on good terms with Narisha." She smiled. "That will get a quick response. Asking about exes usually does."

Alex's phone dinged.

"What did she say?" I asked.

"That Narisha's good stuff, and they're still friends."

"That sounds promising."

Alex shrugged. "We're also asking her ex for input. Maybe not the best source."

"Were they poly when they were together?"

"Let me see," Alex said, typing. She waited a couple of seconds and then said, "Yep, they were."

"Why did they break up?"

Alex looked back at her phone and continued reading. "Ashley says she couldn't handle the scheduling issues of the lifestyle. Narisha spends a lot of time with her primary partner. The breakup was amicable, though."

"I'm glad they're still friends," I said. "Makes me a bit less nervous for our first meeting."

"And we still don't know when that will be," Alex said. "Ask her!"

The truth was that I had been putting it off. Asking out women recently was hard, and I kept having flashbacks to Gen breaking up with me. It was as if my mind was trying to tell me that every potential relationship would end the same way: with the person I love leaving me. I took a deep breath, opened Instagram, and typed a message for her.

> Me: Hi, this is Bells. Mark showed me your
> profile, so I gave it a follow!

I stared at my screen. Gosh, that was cringey.

"I don't think I can send this message," I said.

"Why not?" Alex asked.

"I sound stiff as hell."

"Just send it," Alex replied. "I'm sure she'll understand. We all get nervous."

Despite my better judgment, I sent it. Her reply came back right away.

> Narisha: Hey! Yeah, Mark mentioned you to me. He said you were an impressive gal. Based on your photos, that seems to be true.

"Oh." My cheeks warmed. "She said she likes my pictures."

"That's great!" Alex cheered.

I blinked away the pain from the migraine. The stress from talking to Narisha was making it worse. "I think I need to put my phone away for now. My head is killing me."

"That's okay, check it later," she said. "Why don't you go home and get some rest? We've had enough excitement for one day."

"Sounds great," I said.

Alex drove me home and helped me walk up to my apartment, even though I told her the migraine was a bit better and I didn't need her help. There had been a time when I saw this helpfulness as a sign of romantic attention, but it turned out that there wasn't anything romantic between us. Besides, she was way too intense to date. So, we stayed friends.

Alex was only satisfied once I was safely on the couch with a bottle of water and a blanket.

"There. Don't move from this couch until you feel better," she said. "And take more ibuprofen."

"Okay, Mom," I said sarcastically.

She swatted at me. "Don't call me that. I'm just looking out for you."

"I know, I know. You care about me. It's very nice." I winked. "Now get out of my apartment."

Before I took a much-needed nap, I decided to look at my phone again. There was another message from Narisha waiting for me.

Narisha: Want to meet up on Thursday?
Me: I'd love to!
Narisha: I can't wait to get to know you.

I figured we'd sort the details out later. I went to sleep with a smile on my face.

Chapter
FOUR

On Thursday, I had my date with Narisha. I was nervous. I had spent the better part of the morning scrolling through her Instagram feed. She was seemingly flawless on top of being cool and put together. We had chatted a little back and forth, but it only made her more mysterious.

We were going to the beach. It was her idea. She said she knew the best secluded spots for us to choose from. I liked the beach, but I wasn't a connoisseur, so I deferred to her judgment. By her Instagram, she certainly spent enough time at the beach to know.

We met up at 2:00 in the afternoon, which gave me enough time to worry over my hair and which bathing suit I was going to wear. Today, I definitely cared about my appearance. It was my first real date since me and Gen broke up. That added another level of pressure to meeting Narisha. Plus, it was my first time going out on a date with a polyamorous person.

The beach was surrounded by stones with a path that led directly to the ocean. The sand was warm under my toes. Narisha was waiting for me by the water. There was a small crowd of people lounging by the ocean. I spotted her first from behind. I wasn't certain it was her, as she was gazing out at the water, but her hip-length brown hair helped her stand out. It was wavy with darker streaks that caught in the light. She was fit, and her arms and legs were well-sculpted.

Narisha was wearing a revealing yellow bikini. I looked down at myself. I was wearing a white wrap with cherry blossoms on it.

She certainly had me beat in terms of style. I honestly didn't mind. Not even a little.

"Excuse me," I said, approaching the woman in the yellow bikini. "Are you Narisha?"

She turned around and smiled. I recognized her from her profile. "Yes. You must be Bells."

"Nice to meet you," I said. I wasn't sure if I should shake her hand or not, so instead, I rubbed my arm awkwardly. I could barely form thoughts, let alone words.

"Have you been here long?" she asked.

"No, I found you pretty quickly," I said. Without thinking, I added, "You stand out."

"Oh?" she said, tilting her head. "Do I?"

"Your bathing suit is really bright," I said.

She smiled mischievously. "Is it because of how revealing it is?"

I blushed. "Well, that might have something to do with it."

She smiled. "Did I make a good impression?"

My goodness, she was forward. "Yes. You look great."

"Thank you," she said.

"But you already made a good impression based on your social media. You have so many stunning pictures up there."

"You know, you'd make a great model, too," she said.

"Me?" I asked. "I never thought I would have the 'look' for it."

"You totally do. I could even take your picture sometime if you'd like."

I don't know if it was the way she suggested it—with that smile of hers—or if it was the thought of having her look at me for an extended period, but it made me feel good.

"That'd be great," I said. "I don't know too many female photographers."

"There aren't many of us around," Narisha said, flipping her hair over her shoulder. I noticed the sheen of sweat on her skin. "But I'd be glad to shoot you when we're both free."

"Sure," I said, feeling dazed. I was flattered that a woman like her wanted to spend time making art of me.

"Let me show you the best spot," she said, taking my hand. "Come on!"

"Okay," I said, staring at our intertwined fingers.

I had never held hands with someone within minutes of meeting them, but I really didn't mind.

In fact, I'd be okay with more touching.

She guided me along the beach, past rows of lounging people on towels. Our feet splashed in the water. Eventually, we arrived at our destination. It was on a hill. It was a small, secluded cove, but it had a decent amount of sun and a great ocean view.

"This is a nice spot," I noted.

"I came here earlier to drop this off," she said, motioning to her bag.

I was surprised. "You left a bag here unattended?"

"Nobody ever comes out here. Even if they did, they'd just be stealing our lunch."

"Oh?"

She pulled a bottle of wine, crackers, and cheese from her bag. "It's only a small lunch."

"Thanks for bringing snacks. I would've brought something too if I had known."

"Don't worry about it." She took out two glasses from the bag and poured me some wine. She handed me my glass. "I figured I should show you how you deserve to be treated."

I frowned. "Why do you say that? Did Mark tell you something about my breakup?"

She hesitated. "Well, he mentioned you had been feeling down..."

"I wish he hadn't told you that," I said. "I'd rather tell you things myself."

"Thankfully, now I don't need to ask him questions to get to know you better," she said, seeming reassured. "I can just ask you now that I have you all to myself."

The way she said "all to myself" seemed sensual somehow, although I'm sure she didn't mean it that way. I blamed the self-isolation.

"If you have any more questions, ask away," I said.

"Have you never dated a polyamorous person?" she asked. She adjusted the way she sat so her arm pressed into her chest and accentuated her curves. Her bikini was going to be a distraction.

"Never," I said. "Unless you count Mark."

"I don't count that since you're not in a relationship," she said. "You think that you'd be all right with that kind of lifestyle?"

"Honestly, I don't know," I said. "I think I might be okay with it. I've never tried, though."

"What makes you think you'd be okay with it?"

"I've had feelings for multiple people at once," I replied. "To me, that was evidence that I should explore the lifestyle. I don't know if that's a good reason to try it out, though."

"It's a good reason to think about it." She smiled. "Though I think the real indicator will be whether or not you feel compersion."

"What's that?" I asked.

"It's the opposite of jealousy," she said. "It's when you're happy for your partner when they're with someone else."

"Feeling... happy for them?" I repeated.

"Yes," she said. "It's kind of like being happy for your best friend when they get into a relationship, except you're dating that person."

"Isn't that kind of uncomfortable?" I asked. It was difficult to imagine sitting in the living room, listening to my partner regale me with tales of their date with another person and feeling happy for them.

"It can be uncomfortable if you're prone to jealousy," she said. "But once you work past that, it's totally possible to feel happy for them. It's nice to see the people you care about in love."

"Even when they're not in love with you?" I asked.

"Yes, even then," she said. She propped her chin onto her hand. "But enough serious talk. Tell me more about you."

"I'm a painter," I said. "As you probably saw from my Instagram."

"I did," she said. "I love your use of gold in your art. It's really striking."

I noticed she was wearing gold eyeshadow. It really made her eyes pop. "It's one of my favourite colours."

"I think my favourite paintings of yours were the ones of the witches," she said.

"I always worried that those were too predictable. Pretty colours and pretty women."

"Nothing wrong with enjoying pretty women," she said, sipping her wine.

I laughed. "Agreed."

"Now you ask me a question," she said.

I thought for a moment. "Why did you decide to go to the beach for our first date?"

"So I could get a look at your body and show off mine, obviously," she said, laughing. Her laugh was loud and genuine. I liked the way it lit her face. "But really, it's because I find it's a romantic spot."

"I hope you like what you see," I said. I wasn't usually so forward, but she inspired me. I had to try hard if I wanted to keep up with her.

"I do," she said, a single strand of hair falling across her face. "I like it a lot. You're even more gorgeous in person."

"Well, that's a glowing review," I said, trying to mask my embarrassment at being complimented. "I'm feeling a bit inadequate next to a goddess like you."

"I'm hardly a goddess," she replied, but she seemed pleased by my compliment. "You haven't had any wine. Do you not drink?"

"Oh!" I took a sip of my wine. "No, no. I drink wine. I like it a lot, actually. And this one is really good! I've just been too distracted by you to notice it." I took a few crackers for good measure to prove her efforts at bringing lunch for us weren't wasted.

"I'm sorry for being so distracting," she said, though I knew she wasn't sorry at all. "My turn to ask a question. What do you look for in a partner?"

"Wow, that's a tough question!"

"I like to ask the tough questions upfront," she said. "No point in wasting time."

"Were you worried I'd waste your time because I've never been polyamorous?" I asked.

"A little," she admitted. "But I saw a lot of potential in you. And the fact that you expressed interest in being poly was enough for me. So, back to my question. What do you look for in a partner?"

"I guess I look for someone strong, someone who will commit to me and be loyal. Someone with whom I can be intimate. Someone who can be my best friend."

"That sounds nice."

"What about you?" I asked.

"I look for someone open-minded and interested in experiencing new things."

"That's it?" I asked. It seemed like a pretty short list.

"No, but it's a start," she said. "I also think it's important for me to date someone compassionate and understanding. Compassion goes a long way in relationships."

"I can agree with that," I said, thinking about how Gen had dumped me. She had left me for someone else, discarding me like I meant nothing. That hadn't seemed compassionate. Then again, she didn't seem to care. It occurred to me I hadn't asked about Narisha's love life. "What are your other partners like?"

"I have one partner," she said. "Her name is Eliza. She's off working right now, so we don't see much of each other."

"What does she do for work?"

"She works at the university," Narisha said. "It's a pretty time-consuming job."

"Sounds like it," I said. "How did you two meet?"

"We worked together on a project at the university," she said. "Once it was all over, I asked her out for a glass of wine, and she accepted."

"I'd say I was shocked by your boldness, but I'm not really that surprised," I said.

"Yeah, it was pretty risky," Narisha said. "It was like asking a former manager out on a date."

"But it worked out," I observed.

"Yeah," Narisha said. "I was a bit worried about everything working out at first since she works in HR, and I worked at the university as a TA."

"How did the school react when you told them about your relationship?" I asked.

"We filed some paperwork, made promises, and now it's all officially approved," she said. "We'll never work together again. Thankfully, her job is far removed from the field of psychology. Basically, our relationship won't affect our work anymore, so it's fine."

"I'm glad you two were able to work it out," I said.

"Me too," Narisha replied. "She's a wonderful partner. She's always been there for me when I needed her. We have a lot of fun together. She keeps me grounded, though."

"How so?"

"When I get too impulsive, she's there to rationalize things with me," she said. "Like when we were vacationing in France. I wanted to explore without a plan. But she was wiser and came up with an itinerary for us."

"Sounds like you balance each other out," I said.

"I like to think so." She brushed some sand off her lap. "Eliza is my rock. I really hope that if you two meet, you'll get along. But I'm getting ahead of myself. As for other partners, I don't really consider Mark a partner. You know him as well as I do, I imagine. He's not really into the whole romantic relationship thing."

I laughed. "It's kind of weird, isn't it? The fact that we've both dated him, and he's the one who set us up today."

"It is, yeah," she said. "But you stop caring about the weird after a while when you're poly. Most things about this lifestyle are outside the norm. Besides, if I avoided every person who's slept with one of my partners, I'd never date again. The community is really small, especially for queer women."

"Is that how you identify?" I asked. "As queer?"

"Yes," she said. "I date everyone."

"So, was Mark a fling or something else?" I asked.

"He's fun," she said. "But I'm looking for a lot more than just fun."

"Oh?" I asked. "So you're looking for something serious?"

"Yeah," she replied, pushing her hair out of her face. "I don't really do casual relationships. When I get serious about someone, I get *really* serious."

"That's interesting, given that you have a primary partner," I said. I felt the same way about relationships.

"What do you mean by that?"

"I figured having a primary partner would mean you can't get very close to the other people you date."

"Not at all," she replied. "I get close to the people I date. But I can't get close to too many at once. I find I get overwhelmed if I date more than two people."

How do I tell her that I fell in love fast and hard? That, like her, I said yes to new experiences. How could I tell her I wanted to kiss her more than anything else right now?

"I just thought you should know that in case things work out between us," she said, which seemed rather presumptuous, but I didn't care. My mind was in the same place. I was already imagining what we would look like as a couple, and we hadn't even kissed yet.

"Do you find you get serious about people fast, too?" she asked.

I wondered if it was a leading question. What if Mark had already warned her about how intense I get when I become infatuated? Meeting through a mutual friend was certainly one way to dispel the mystery about another person.

"I do," I said.

"It happens like that for me, too," she said.

"I hope it's not impolite of me to ask, but how does it work," I asked, "when you fall in love with someone hard and fast in polyamory? Because there's more than one person. How can you focus on your feelings for them when you have other things going on?"

"Each relationship is different," Narisha replied. "Just because I have a primary partner doesn't mean I don't get excited about my other partners, too."

I laughed. "There's just so much to think about. Everything is so new to me."

"That's understandable. I was overwhelmed at first, too."

"But you seem so confident about it all!" I exclaimed.

"When I started my poly lifestyle, I made a lot of mistakes. Hurt people's feelings. It was only after a few years of reading, talking, and experiencing things that I finally started to feel more comfortable with it all."

I was impressed with her for admitting that. Most people weren't upfront about their flaws. She seemed to put it all on the table: both her successes and her failures.

"I guess I did the same thing with monogamous dating," I said. "I messed up and hurt people's feelings too, mostly because I didn't know how to communicate."

"It can apply to either polyamory or monogamy," she said. "So don't be too hard on yourself. Almost everyone gets off to a rocky start. It's not always a smooth transition."

"No, I imagine not," I said. I ate a few crackers with cheese. Narisha poured herself more wine.

"Mark mentioned you're single because you'd experienced heartbreak. Can I ask what happened?"

I was stunned. That was a bold question to ask. Plus, it was considered bad form to ask someone about their exes on the first date. But maybe the poly world worked differently. I took a deep breath.

"She left me for someone else," I said. "It hurts. A lot. I lost my trust in her. So, even though the offer to get back together was tempting, I haven't accepted."

"That's very wise," she mused.

"Except it took my friend Alex and Mark to talk sense into me," I replied. "I was actually considering it at first."

"Love makes us all fools," she said. "Could you see yourself falling for me?"

How many daring questions was she going to ask me today? I considered her question. She was stunning, intelligent, bold, and confident. Could I fall for someone like that?

Of course. But there was also the fact that she liked to date other people. That could be a small issue for me if it turned out I don't fare well with the polyamorous lifestyle.

"Yes," I said. "I think I could."

"I think I could fall for you, too," Narisha said. "I really want to kiss you. Is that okay?"

I was shocked. "Really?"

She nodded.

"I want to kiss you, too," I said.

She kissed me.

This kiss was different from the last time I had been kissed by a woman. With Gen, I had felt insecure. With Narisha, I felt warm and safe. She wrapped her arms around me, and they were surprisingly strong. Her hair smelled wonderful, like coconuts. There were specks of gold on her cheeks from her eyeshadow.

"What was that for?" I asked with a smile.

"Because you're beautiful," she said. "And I felt like it."

"You just say and do what you feel, don't you?" I asked, taking her hand in mine.

"Most of the time," she said. "Is that a problem?"

"Not at all." I brushed my lips against her cheek. "I like it."

"Thanks," she said. "You're pretty great."

"Compared to you, I'm not," I said. "I'm an introverted painter who spends most of her time isolated inside. You're an adventurous photographer with a strong will. We couldn't be more different."

"And yet we both feel this," she said, smoothing my hair away from my face. "I'd say it's worth exploring, wouldn't you?"

"Definitely."

The next four hours flew by. I learned she was from British Columbia. She liked to listen to rock and metal. She worked as a TA in psychology while completing her graduate degree. She took English Literature courses for fun and cared deeply about social issues.

Our date ended once it became colder and we needed to change out of our bathing suits.

We kissed goodbye, and she promised to see me again.

I really hoped that was true because I felt a real connection with her. One that might even lead somewhere.

Chapter
FIVE

Alex and her girlfriend Nina visited my place two weeks after my first date with Narisha. There had been two more since then. They weren't just visiting to ask me about how our dates went—though I was certain that would be a main topic of conversation—but they were coming over mainly to check up on the status of their commission. The painting was half-done, and I didn't mind letting them see my work in progress. I didn't trust most people with my unfinished pieces, but Alex and Nina were good friends. I knew they wouldn't judge me too harshly for an incomplete piece.

They were both sitting on my couch, waiting to see the painting. Alex was dressed in activewear—I rarely saw her wearing anything else. She wore blue yoga pants with pockets and a loose white top that accentuated her biceps. Her blonde hair was pulled back into a ponytail.

Nina almost always dressed well. She wore a long black dress that fell to her ankles, capped with a white collar. Her black hair was curled and fell past her shoulders, while her dark eyeliner accentuated her pale skin. I knew she avoided the sun and mixed white concealer in with her normal makeup to give off a more gothy effect. Alex wasn't as into the goth scene as Nina was, but they made it work.

I hoped she didn't mind Ghost laying on her lap, but the cat was super affectionate. It was hard to deny her.

I brought out the canvas, and Nina gasped audibly.

"It's so beautiful!" she exclaimed, throwing her hands to her mouth.

"It's not exactly done, but I'm glad you like it," I said, feeling a swell of pride.

"I do, I love it!" she said. "I knew when Alex recommended you that you'd be the right person for the job. You did exactly what I wanted! I love her eyes and how vacant they look."

"It's very spooky," Alex said.

"How long until it's done?" Nina asked.

She was practically sitting at the edge of the couch, looking ready to spring to her feet and take the painting from me now. Ghost had moved onto Alex's lap.

"I'd say a few days, depending on how fast I work," I said.

I could probably finish it in one, but I wanted to give myself time in case something came up or I didn't have the inspiration to paint.

"Ah! That's great. I can't wait to hang the finished product in my apartment!" Nina exclaimed gleefully.

"Where do you think you'll put it?" I asked them.

"In the living room," Nina said, while at the same time, Alex said, "In the spare room."

They looked at each other momentarily, and I sensed some tension.

"No, we agreed we'd put it in the living room," Nina said slowly. "Don't you remember?"

"But it's not exactly what I want everyone to see when they come into our home," Alex reproached. "It's kind of creepy."

"It is beautiful!" Nina protested. "Don't you want to display your best friend's art in our home? Or are you ashamed of it?"

Oh boy. I was getting pulled into a couple's fight about home décor.

"I don't think Alex is ashamed of my work. She's always been one of my biggest supporters. I think you two just have different opinions about what should go where. I'm sure, once the painting is done, you'll have a better idea about where you want to put it."

That seemed to reassure Nina. "True. It's not even finished yet. We're thinking too far ahead."

Alex mouthed, "Thank you."

I smiled. "Just be patient, and I'll do my best to make it turn out exactly the way you want." I turned my attention back to the canvas. "Is there anything you'd like me to change? It's not too late."

Nina paused for a few moments, studying the painting. "No, I think it's great the way it is. You really nailed it."

I beamed. "Thank you." I placed the canvas back on an easel.

"With that out of the way," Alex said, petting Ghost on the head, "how did your last date with Narisha go?"

"Oh, that?" I laughed nervously. Even thinking about her was enough to raise my heart rate. "It went really, really well. We've been texting almost nonstop. For our second date, we went to a café. For our third, she took me out for pho. I think she's amazing."

"Wow," Nina said. "That's great. But aren't you afraid you're moving too fast? You're still so new to the polyamory thing, after all..."

"Honey, I don't think we can really criticize her for moving too fast," Alex said. "You and I got together after a single date. They've been talking for two weeks."

Nina blushed. "I suppose that's true."

Alex turned to look at me gleefully. "Give me details! I want to know everything about this woman. What is she like?"

"She said she asked me to go to the beach with her on the first date so she could see what I looked like in a swimsuit."

"Oh! That's sneaky," Alex said. "I bet she's beautiful."

"She is," I said. "I mean, you've seen her Instagram profile."

"I haven't seen her Instagram!" Nina said. "Let me see, too."

Alex pulled out her phone and showed her. The more she scrolled through her profile, the wider Nina's eyes became.

"Oh. I get it now," Nina said.

"Exactly." I sighed and sat on the chair in front of them. "She's great. We spent some time listening to music in her car. We have a lot of the same tastes. It was fun singing along with her."

"She seems like a good fit for you," Nina said.

"When I'm by her side, I'm in awe of her. I feel like she's a bit too far out of my league."

"Don't think of it that way," Nina said. "If she likes you, that's all that matters."

"And?" Alex asked. "*Does* she like you?"

I thought back to our first kiss and how wonderful it had felt. The sun had been shining on my face, and I had felt her smile pressed against my lips. I thought of the nights we spent on the phone talking about our dreams for the future. I also thought about how many times she told me she appreciated meeting me.

"She likes me, yes."

"That's great, then," Alex said. "Though I still don't know if the polyamory thing is right for you."

"Me neither," I said. "But I guess we'll find out."

"Have you been seeing Mark regularly, as well?" Alex asked.

"I've seen him twice a week," I said. "I didn't stay over this time, though."

"What did you guys get up to?"

"We watched movies and played video games, mostly."

"Has he been out on many dates lately?" Nina asked.

"He's been out on a few," I replied.

"I could never have a poly relationship," Nina said. "I get jealous way too easily."

"According to Narisha, there's a feeling called 'compersion,' which is the opposite of jealousy," I said. "It means feeling happy for your partner when they're with someone else."

Nina gasped. "Really? That's a thing?"

"Really."

"Well, at least you know what you're getting yourself into," Alex said. "Seems like she made herself pretty clear from the get-go."

"She did, yeah," I said. I was excited, but I was also nervous. "We've kissed."

"How was it?" Nina asked.

"It was really nice," I said.

"Have you told Gen you're not interested?" Alex asked. "She's probably still waiting for your answer."

I looked at my pocket, where my phone was. "No. I haven't."

"Why not?"

"I honestly haven't wanted to deal with it," I muttered. "I figured my silence would speak for itself."

"I think it would give you a sense of closure, wouldn't it?" she asked.

"Yeah. It would." I shrugged. "I just didn't want to have to talk to her again."

"It would probably save you future headaches to deal with Gen now," Alex said. "Rather than waiting for later."

Nina looked at me sympathetically. They both waited for my answer. Clearly, this is something they had discussed before coming over. They wanted me to talk to Gen and tell her I wasn't interested in dating her again.

"Fine," I breathed. "I'll talk to her."

"I think that's for the best," Nina said. "That way, she won't be able to try and get back together with you again."

"She doesn't deserve you," Alex added. "She left you for someone else and then regretted her choice. Which sucks for her. But she needs to live with it."

"You're right," I said. It still stung to think of her betrayal. "I'll deal with it."

"I'm sure you'll feel better once it's done," Alex said. "And Nina and I are always here for you if you need us."

"Thanks, guys," I said.

"No, thank you for letting us come view the painting before it's done," Nina said. "I appreciate all your hard work."

"You're welcome," I said, but my thoughts were elsewhere. I was steeling myself for the phone call I was about to make to Gen. "I'll do my best to get it done soon."

Alex put the cat on the floor, stood from her seat, and hugged me. "I'm glad today went so well, Bells. Keep me updated."

I hugged her back and said goodbye to Nina. Once they were gone, I collapsed onto the couch and pulled out my phone. Why was this phone call making me so nervous? Even just pulling up Gen's number made my heart race. My friends had confirmed it: she was trying to take advantage of me by offering a polyamorous arrangement. Even though the whole poly thing wasn't as bad as I had originally thought, I knew I didn't want to do it with her. It was either monogamy or nothing else. I couldn't trust her after she left me for her now ex-boyfriend.

If she offered monogamy, would I accept it? I remembered how I felt at the café when she told me she still loved me. I was relieved. But that had been a naïve reaction. Getting back together with her would only prolong the inevitable. Gen wasn't loyal to me. She had already proven that. Whether we were in an open relationship or not, she would probably leave me for someone else. That, or I would never take priority. It would be the next newest, shiniest person.

So, no. If she offered a monogamous relationship, I wouldn't take it.

It was clear to me that no relationship was possible between us.

I called her. It rang twice before she picked up. She sounded hopeful. "Hello?"

"Hi," I said. "It's Bells."

"I know," she said. "I have Caller ID."

"Right." God, how had I already made this so awkward? "I'm calling because I wanted to talk about your offer to get back together."

"Sure," she said breathlessly. "I'm just out for a walk."

I thought of her out for a walk with her adorable dachshund. Did I really want to tell her this vital piece of information while she was out? What if she started crying in the park? Did I really want to have this conversation now?

She needed to know.

"I don't think I can do it," I said quietly.

"What?" I think she stopped walking. I couldn't hear her footsteps anymore. "Why not?"

"Because you left me, and I don't think I have it in me to trust you entirely," I said.

"But you told me at the café that you forgave me!" she exclaimed.

"I know I did, and I do. I forgive you. I won't hold a grudge against you." I was surprised by how firm I was. I had half-expected myself to just give in to her demands like always. But I wasn't going to be a pushover anymore. I was going to be an adult, and I was going to set some boundaries. "But I also can't put myself back in that vulnerable position again."

"I know polyamory can be intimidating. And I know you'll feel vulnerable often. But you can trust me. I won't hurt you again. That was a one-time mistake. What happened with Nate won't ever happen again."

"It's not the polyamory," I said quietly. "I'm actually coming around to that. What I can't tolerate is the thought of trusting you again."

"Seriously?" I could hear her breath coming quickly now. She was getting worked up. "Is there someone else?"

My chest tightened. "Why would you ask that?"

"Because you're suddenly fine with the polyamory part, but not me," she said. "Meaning that someone else convinced you polyamory is okay."

"No," I said weakly. "I just had a lot of time to think about it, and I came around to the idea."

"I doubt you came to that conclusion alone," she said. Now that she wasn't getting what she wanted, she dropped the nice act. "So, who is she? Assuming it's a woman, of course."

I didn't answer. I didn't know how. Why did she deserve to know about Narisha? Or Mark, for that matter? It was awfully presumptuous of her to assume anything about the new people I was seeing.

"Whether or not I'm seeing someone isn't important," I said. "I'm calling to talk about you and me."

"Yeah, which apparently doesn't exist now," she said. "If what you're telling me is true, then our relationship is over."

"Our relationship was over the minute you left me for someone else!" I exclaimed, perhaps a bit too forcefully.

There was silence on the other end for a few moments, and then, "Fair. I had just hoped that there was a future between us."

"The only future I can foresee between us is as friends," I said. "I don't think I can do anything more."

"Because I left you."

"Yes," I said.

"I'm sad you won't forgive me for that," Gen said. "I apologized. I told you I still loved you. Why isn't that enough?"

"Because it's not," I said. "It's just not. You can't just break someone's trust like that and expect them to return easily."

"None of this has been easy! But I thought I was worth the effort. I thought *we* were worth the effort."

"Not when it ends like it did last time," I said. "I'm sorry."

I heard her sniffle. "Okay, I need to know. Please tell me. Who is this other person? Why are they so special that you'll consider having a relationship with them and not me?"

I don't know why I decided to be honest with her. Maybe it was because of how pathetic she sounded on the other end of the line. She was out for a walk with her dog, and now she was crying in public, all because of me. The least I could do was be honest.

"I'm seeing someone new. Her name is Narisha. And she's polyamorous. She has been for a while now. She understands it way better than me."

"So that's it? You're just going to ditch me and try polyamory with someone new? Someone you barely even know?"

"At least I might be able to trust her," I shot back. I realized, after I said it, that was a low blow. Gen didn't need me tearing her down right now. "I'm sorry. That was rude of me."

"It's fine, I know we're both emotional right now," Gen said. "I just can't believe you're choosing someone else over me."

"I know rejection is hard," I said. "But I can't be with you romantically. I'm sorry."

"You know, her name sounds familiar," Gen said. "Narisha... I've heard that name before."

Part of me wanted to hang up as soon as she said that. I didn't need more drama in my life right now. If Gen somehow had connections to Narisha, I didn't want to know about them. I didn't want to spend every future date with her worrying about Gen finding out what we did. Because I knew Gen would be looking for info on us.

"Oh, I know!" she said. "I know someone that was dating her. Ashley."

I had heard this name twice now. Ashley. She was the woman that Alex knew, the one she had texted for information on Narisha. "They're not seeing each other anymore."

"No," Gen said. "Because Ashley is seeing me now."

It was my turn to be stunned. "What?"

"I started seeing Ashley," Gen said. "Recently."

Obviously it had to be recent! Gen was asking me to get back together with her only a couple weeks ago! She told me her focus would be on me. That clearly wasn't true. How had she found time to get a new partner in just a couple weeks? I was upset, but I couldn't rightfully be angry with her because she wasn't my girlfriend. We weren't even dating anymore. So, why did I feel like she had betrayed me again?

"Oh," was all I managed to say.

"The poly world is a small one," Gen said. "Especially the sapphic part. We'll all probably run into each other eventually."

I bit my lip to force back the words I wanted to say. I wanted to accuse her of being untrustworthy, of moving too fast, and of not caring about my emotions. I wanted to accuse her of so much, but instead, I bit it down.

"I'm glad you found someone, then," was all I managed to say.

"Don't say it like that. It's not like she was a replacement for you."

I wanted to point out that she was the one who used the word 'replacement,' not me, but I thought better of it.

"It seems like you move on fast," she remarked.

"So do you," I replied pointedly.

We were taking passes at each other now. Great.

"Look, if there's nothing else to say, I should really go," I said. Not the smoothest exit of my life, but I didn't know how else to end the conversation. I felt stressed, upset, and sad. I wished I could throw my phone out the window and never think about Gen again.

"I guess there's nothing else to say," Gen said, defeated. "I wish you would reconsider. Because you and I... we could be great together. I wish you'd give us another chance."

"I'm sorry, but I can't," I said. "Goodbye, Gen."

I hung up. I didn't even give her a chance to say bye. I knew she would try to prolong the conversation for as long as possible until she swayed me over to her side of things. I wouldn't have described her as manipulative when we were together, but I could see it now we were broken up. Gen liked to twist people's feelings to suit her desires. Unfortunately for her, I had friends who looked out for me. Friends who knew what was best for me, even when I sometimes didn't.

I needed those friends now more than ever.

One of those friends was particularly helpful after hard times. Mark's physique didn't hurt, either. We might not be emotionally in sync, but we were physically in sync. I stayed the night to make sure we had enough time together.

Once we woke up and got out of bed, we lounged in his kitchen. I had borrowed one of his shirts and was wearing a pair of my best low-rise shorts. I liked how I could dress comfortably when I was around him. With other guys, I usually worried about what I was wearing and if I looked good. With Mark, I could just be myself, and I knew that was enough.

"So, you did it," Mark said, pouring sugar into his freshly made cup of coffee. "I'm proud of you. You stood up for yourself and established some boundaries."

"I did it," I confirmed. "It was hard, but I did it."

"Let me guess, Gen didn't take too well to you asserting yourself," he said, taking a sip from his coffee.

"She was confused and didn't like that I wouldn't give her another chance."

"Makes sense. She didn't get her way, so she was upset," he said.

"And get this: she's dating Narisha's ex, Ashley."

"She's already dating someone else?" he asked, surprised. "Wow. Girl moves fast. I figured she'd probably wait for your answer before moving on. Guess I was wrong."

"Yeah, I was shocked, too," I said. "But it's none of my business."

"Would you like a coffee?"

"No, thank you," I said. "I feel anxious enough without the caffeine."

He took a seat on the stool next to me at the kitchen counter. "So, she's dating Ashley, huh? That's interesting."

"Why is it interesting?" I asked, hoping he couldn't tell how eager I was for more information on her. I wanted to know more about Ashley so I could get to know more about Narisha. They had dated once, after all.

"Because Narisha told me she and Ashley broke up because Ashley was monogamous," he said. "Seems she changed her mind."

I winced. "Ouch. I wonder if Narisha knows that her ex is back into polyamory with someone else."

"She might," Mark said. "But she hasn't mentioned it to me. Have you told her about it?"

"Not yet." I paused. "Are you two still…"

He smiled at me. "Bells, are you really asking me right now if she and I are still sleeping together after what we just did?"

I blushed. "Well, I just… I figured that if she and I got along that, you know, one of us would stop sleeping with you…"

"Only one of you?" he asked, the same smirk still stuck on his face. "And I imagine the person that would keep sleeping with me is you?"

"Well…" I trailed off, aware of how flawed my plan was. "I guess I didn't really think it through."

"For your information, no, we haven't slept together recently. Not since you two met. She's been really busy. I don't know if she's avoiding me or not. But she might find it just as awkward as you to have shared friends-with-benefits."

I had to hold back my sigh of relief. "Oh, I see."

"But you know, part of polyamory is sharing your partner with others. Even your friends. Or friends-with-benefits. If Narisha asks to sleep with me, I'll say yes." He held my gaze. He seemed serious. "How do you feel about that?"

"I understand," I said. "If I'm going to be polyamorous, I have to quickly learn that the rules aren't the same anymore. Sometimes, your friends-with-benefits are also sleeping with the girl that you like. It's a small community. People are bound to know each other."

"Right."

"It still kind of bothers me, though," I said. "I don't know if that's just growing pains or if it's genuinely awkward that we've both kind of dated you."

"Thanks for letting me know how you feel," he said. "I don't think you have to worry about her calling me up any time soon. She's been pretty quiet. When we do talk, she mostly talks about you."

"That's sweet."

"So, how serious is it between you two? You've been on a few dates now, haven't you?"

"Yeah, we have. It's not super serious yet. I don't move *that* fast."

"Yeah, you do."

"Okay, maybe I move a little fast. I just want to be careful with how I treat her. I want her to know that I respect her. I don't want her to feel like I'm just using her as an experiment."

He set his cup down. "And you've spent enough time with her to know?"

"I think so," I said. "I know we don't know each other that well yet, but from what I saw, I'm impressed. And I want to know more. Is that so bad?"

"It's not bad at all," he said. "In fact, I'm happy for you. It's due time that you got out and started flirting again instead of wallowing over sad paintings in your house."

"Not all my paintings are sad," I shot back. "Only some of them."

"Yeah. Especially the ones where you paint your ex-lovers. You know, it's kind of morbid."

"Don't make fun of my creative process."

He smiled. "I'm just teasing you."

"You're lucky I like you," I said, then froze. Shit. Did I just tell Mark that I liked him? I studied his face, wondering if he had caught the double meaning of what I said.

He looked as relaxed as ever, leading me to believe he hadn't read into it. "What's not to like?" he asked playfully. "So, do you and Narisha have another date lined up?"

"Not yet," I said. "But I was planning on asking her about that tonight."

"Good idea," he said. "I think she told me she was going to some event tonight."

"Really?" I felt a twinge of excitement at the thought of seeing her there. I wanted to be wherever she was and do whatever she did. I wanted to be around her and experience the world with her.

"Yeah, it's some kind of art gala. I think one of our friends created the art."

"Oh, cool," I said. "I've probably spent way too much time hiding in my apartment. I didn't hear about this gala at all. If I had, I probably would've planned to go."

"I was thinking of going too," he said pensively.

"You were invited?" I asked. "Don't tell me: you're sleeping with the host, too."

He laughed. "No, but good guess. I'm just friends with the artist. Believe it or not, I have some of those, too. He invited me, but I hadn't decided if I was going. It was honestly between that and going to the gym."

My fingers trembled a little as I said, "We should go together."

"Together?" he repeated. "Like a date?"

"Or like two friends going to an event together," I said quickly. My nerves were getting the best of me.

He considered, tapping his fingers against the kitchen counter. "Hm. True. It would be good for me to go. And if you were there, I wouldn't be alone…"

And I'd be able to see Narisha.

Granted, it would be awkward to have Mark, Narisha, and I all in one spot, but maybe it was best to face my fears. Maybe, once I saw Mark and Narisha interact face to face, I wouldn't feel so uncomfortable. He didn't do romantic relationships, after all. And he was the one who set us up. But still, I had this fear deep down that they would leave me for each other. It was probably some leftover trauma from my breakup. Having all of us hang out at the art gallery could remind me that not everyone would leave me.

"All right, let's do it," he said. "Let's go together. It'll be fun."

"Great!" I said. "I'll tell Narisha."

I pulled out my phone to text her.

> Me: I heard you were going to an art gallery tonight. I'll be there too, with Mark!

```
Narisha: Really? I'm so pumped to be able to
see you again :D
Me: I  know  we  only  just  saw  each  other
recently,  but  I'm  pumped  to  see  you,  too.
There's  so  much  I  want  to  know  about  you.
```

I wasn't certain if that last part was a bit too sappy or not. But she took it well.

```
Narisha:  I  want  to  know  more  about  you,  too
:)  Maybe  we  can  get  to  know  each  other  better
tonight  at  the  gallery.
Me:  I'd  like  that.
```

"Is she excited you're coming?" Mark asked, leaning toward me to read over my shoulder.

"Yep!" I said, putting my phone in my pocket. "She says she looks forward to getting to know me better."

"That's great!" Mark said. He stood and placed his hands on my hips suggestively. "And you know, there's still time for us to get to know each other a little better before the event…"

I laughed. "I would hope so. There's still several hours before we have to go."

"That's plenty of time," he said before kissing my neck.

I melted into his touch. Despite how heavenly it felt, I was distracted. I liked Narisha, and even texting her had given me a rush of excitement. But now, Mark was here, and he was kissing me. And the weirdest part was that she knew about that and was totally okay with it. She didn't mind that I was hooking up with him.

Even still, I had this lingering feeling of guilt, like I was doing something wrong. I knew everyone was open about their relationships with one another and that I wasn't going behind anyone's back, but I was still nervous. I had gone on a few great dates with Narisha, and I didn't want to do anything to mess it up. I had been monogamous for so long that kissing Mark felt like I was betraying her. But there was a new way of thinking. A polyamorous way of thinking. And that way of thinking told me it was okay to kiss Mark and Narisha if they both knew about it.

Though my rational side knew this, my emotional side didn't quite understand. I felt dazed and confused. I closed my mouth and sat back.

"I'm sorry," I said, covering my face with my hands. "I think I just need a second."

"Is something wrong?" Mark asked, sitting back down.

I sighed. "I think I'm having a difficult time wrapping my head around this poly stuff."

"Ohh," he said. "I get it."

"I know that Narisha and I only went on a few dates, but I really like her," I said. "I'm so accustomed to cuffing myself to the first person I like."

"So, you're saying it's a bit weird to kiss me when you know you like someone else?"

I shrugged. "Basically, yeah. Sorry."

"You don't need to apologize," he said. "I think that's natural, especially when you've been monogamous your whole life."

"It is?"

He nodded. "Definitely."

I shook my head. "I don't know what's wrong with me. Narisha knows about you. She approves of my relationship with you. I think she even *likes* that I'm seeing you. She told me about this thing called compersion, where you're happy for your partner when they're with someone else they like. But even though I know all of this, I still feel like I'm cheating on her or something. Like I'm doing something wrong."

"You're not doing anything wrong," Mark said. "And you're right, she probably is happy that we're seeing each other like this. Her life philosophy seems to be 'the more, the merrier.'"

"It's all just so... different," I said, not wanting to call it something offensive. I knew that, for some people, it was the norm, but it was already challenging so many beliefs about relationships that I had. "How are you adjusting to the polyamorous label?"

"I think I might prefer non-monogamous," Mark said. "I've been thinking on it. There's a slight difference."

"What's that?"

"Well, polyamory is when you love multiple people." He got up, went to the fridge, and pulled out a yogurt cup. "I don't really get into relationships or fall in love. I can't really call myself poly, so I call myself non-monogamous instead."

"Interesting. I've never thought of it that way."

He took a spoon from the drawer and ate his yogurt. "Stick with me, kid, and you'll learn a lot."

I laughed. "Whatever."

"But seriously, if you'd prefer we didn't kiss for the rest of the day, I can do that," he said. "I just want you to be comfortable."

I loved how considerate he was. It was one of my favourite things about him.

"Thank you," I said. "But I should be fine. I need to get accustomed to how this works."

"I'm glad you said that," he said, and pulled me into his arms.

Chapter
SIX

Mark and I took a cab to the event. We walked in together, arm in arm. Narisha was already standing near the entrance dressed in a sparkling blue gown that fell to her feet. The back of the dress was mostly straps. Seeing the curve of her back seemed intimate. Her hair was curled, and she had applied a smokey makeup look to her eyes. She was stunning. I was dressed in black leather pants and a green dress shirt with a plunging neckline. Mark had worn dress pants, a dress shirt, and a tie. His hair was a fashioned mess. His look gave the impression he'd only spent ten minutes on it, and yet he appeared stylish.

"Welcome," she said to us as we entered the gallery. She kissed us each on the cheek. "Glad to see you both."

From the entrance, we could see several art pieces hanging up on the wall. They were all brightly coloured mermaids. Some were lounging on rocks, while others had their tails coiled around them underwater. From what I could see from the doors, it looked incredible.

"I'm glad to see you too," I said. Her kissing us both made me more aware of how she was technically dating both of us.

"Would you like some wine?" she asked, indicating her glass.

"No, thank you," Mark said.

"I'm good," I said quietly. I was sure if I drank any wine right now, my nerves would make me open my big mouth and say something embarrassing. I wanted to make a good impression on her tonight.

"Here it is," she said, motioning to the walls.

They were digital paintings, each featuring a mermaid. Some of them were beautiful and serene, while others were dark and haunting. This project had apparently been born out of a Twitter hashtag in May.

"Digital art is my medium, so I should appreciate the talent at work here," Mark said.

I looked at the painting closest to us. "It's pretty," I said, knowing I should say more but feeling at a loss for words. I was nervous.

"I thought you would like it," she said, beaming. She winked at me. "I especially liked the framing. The subjects are in focus, with so much going on around them."

"Oh! You're right." I said.

We walked through the rows of paintings. Mark motioned to one of a mermaid with the tail of a shark. "This one has to be my favourite. Not only because sharks are cool but also because the brushwork here is insane. I love it."

"It's really nice," I agreed.

"Not as nice as you," Narisha said.

"All right, all right." Mark smiled. "Enough flirting. I'm here too, you know!"

"Aww, is Mark feeling left out?" Narisha asked, then shoved him playfully on the shoulder. "No need for that."

I laughed. Was it really this easy? Could all three of us meet in one place like this without anger or jealousy? It was hard to believe. I felt like Narisha could make a passive-aggressive comment about me and Mark any minute now. But she didn't. It was all in my head.

We moved from the entrance and stood before the first piece. It depicted two mermaids with their tails intertwined. They gazed at each other longingly.

"That's pretty sapphic," I observed.

"Yeah," Narisha said and slipped her hand into mine. "It is."

I resisted the urge to look at Mark's reaction. He was behind us, so I'd have to turn around to see, and that would make things awkward with her hand in mine. I could only assume he was okay with it. He moved to stand beside me.

"How does it feel to be here with both of us?" Mark asked.

"It's different," I said. "But I like how everyone is getting along."

"Of course we are." He smiled. "Why don't I give you two some time alone? I'll go over and talk to the artist and congratulate him on their good work."

"Sounds good," Narisha said.

I was relieved to finally be alone with her. We hadn't had much time to see each other after our last date. Most of our interactions had been limited to our phones.

"Are you really okay with us both being here?" Narisha asked. Her eyes were wide with concern. "I know it's a lot."

"I'm okay with it, but you're right: it is a lot." I laughed. "I didn't really think it through properly. I just figured if I was okay with being polyamorous, then I should be okay with having you both in the same room. Turns out it was a bit more stressful than I imagined."

"It's okay," Narisha said. "When you texted me and told me you'd be coming with Mark, I thought of warning you. But I didn't want you to think I was telling you what to do."

"I appreciate that," I said. "I wouldn't have seen it that way. I would have seen it as thoughtful advice from someone with more experience than me."

"It seems Mark caught the vibe, anyway." She motioned to where he stood a few feet away, talking animatedly with the artist, Matt. "It's not always easy being a metamour, you know."

"A what?"

"A metamour," she repeated. "It means you're connected to someone through their lover. That you're both dating them."

"Except he's not just my metamour," I said. "He's also my... well, he's like a partner."

"Yeah," she said. "I know it's all a bit awkward. But I think it's very mature of you to agree to visit the art gala with him tonight."

"Why wouldn't I?" I asked. "I wanted to see you. I liked seeing Mark. I thought we could all see each other."

"I think you're brave for fighting that fear and coming here anyway."

"You think I'm brave?" I grinned. "Thank you."

"I think what you're doing takes a lot of courage. Most people wouldn't be able to meet like this. Emotions can get complicated."

"Consider me uncomplicated, then," I said.

"Oh no," Narisha said. "I think this is a little complicated. But that's not a bad thing. I like it."

"Well, polyamory is better than I imagined."

"Yeah? What brought you around to it?" she asked.

"I don't know. I think it's something about you and Mark. You both put me at ease." I smiled. "With you two, I feel safe."

"That's because you can trust us," she said. "We're here for you."

"I know," I said. "And the fact that I know you're both there for me, and that you have my back, means the world."

"It means a lot to me, too," she said with a small smile.

We continued to view the art, and I eventually took a glass of wine. I was especially taken by a piece depicting a mermaid with a brightly coloured tail. It almost seemed to sparkle in the light. Her hair was long and auburn-coloured. Her lips were red and parted slightly. Waves crashed around her. She rose from the water, her tail partially submerged in the foam. It was a beautiful painting.

"I like this one the best," I declared as we stood before it.

"It's pretty good, isn't it?" Mark asked, sliding in beside me. He turned to Narisha. "Sorry for being gone for so long. Have you both been enjoying yourselves?"

"Yes. The art is wonderful, and the company is even better," I said.

"That's good to hear," he replied.

"Oh! And Narisha taught me a new word: metamour."

"Oh, right. That one means... the lover of your lover, right?" he asked.

Narisha nodded. "That's right. And given how we're all connected to each other..."

He ran a hand through his hair. "God, that's all a bit messy now, isn't it?"

"Yeah, but at least we're all on board with it," I observed.

"True," he said. "I suppose it would be worse if one of us wasn't pleased with the arrangement."

Looking at Mark and Narisha standing together, I couldn't help but imagine them in a more intimate setting. How did she act when they were in private? Was she a whole other person, or was she exactly the same as she was now? Jealousy pushed at the edge of my consciousness, but I tried to ignore it. It wouldn't help to be jealous right now.

Besides, Narisha and Mark were strictly casual. They were no different from me and him, which worried me, too. I liked him. Who's to say Narisha didn't secretly harbour affections for him, too? I tried to imagine it.

"You know," I began nervously. "You two don't have to hold back because of me."

"Hold back?" Mark asked, surprised. "What do you mean?"

"I mean, she's been holding my hand a lot tonight, and she hasn't touched yours. And I thought you both might be holding back on my account. If that's the case, you shouldn't. I need to get accustomed to the whole polyamory thing, and besides, I already know you two are seeing each other."

Narisha looked like she was holding back a laugh. "You're saying you... want me to hold hands with Mark?"

Her tone was incredulous. I motioned to them, standing next to each other.

"If you want to. I know you're both seeing each other. You don't have to hide it from me."

"We're not hiding anything," Mark said. "This is just how we act when we're together. We don't really do public displays of affection. It's not that different from me and you. If we were out together, we wouldn't hold hands, right?"

"Right," I repeated. "I just don't want you to worry about that…"

"Not at all," Narisha said. "Mark's not lying to spare your feelings. It's the truth. We don't do PDA. It's not our thing. We're not even really dating. So, you see, we're not holding back at all."

"I'm glad, then," I said.

I felt relieved. That was one less thing I had to worry about tonight. I didn't want them treating me with extreme caution just because I was new to polyamory.

"I think I'm going to buy a painting," Narisha announced.

"Really?" Mark asked. "There are so many great ones."

"I know," she replied. "And I want to support Matt as much as possible. So, that means I'll be buying one of his paintings tonight."

I peeked at the price tag beneath the painting in front of us. It was pricey for an evening out with friends. I was surprised Narisha had enough money to buy things so easily, but, then again, I didn't know much about her personal finances.

"Which one will you be getting?" I asked.

She pointed to the painting before us. The one I said I liked with the waves surrounding her.

"That one."

"Good choice," I said.

She turned to me and grinned. "And I'm going to be giving it to you."

"To me?" I repeated. I raised my hands. "Oh no, I couldn't. That's way too expensive."

"I'm going to buy a painting one way or another tonight. What does it matter if I give it to you?" she asked.

"Because you deserve to keep something so precious," I insisted. "I really don't deserve a gift that nice."

"Oh, but you do," she said and kissed me on the cheek. "I know you really wanted it, and I can afford it. Why not let me get it for you?"

I looked over Narisha's shoulder at Mark. He nodded enthusiastically. I didn't know what to do. It was too generous of her to offer me such a pricey gift. And this wasn't even a real date. I had just shown up at the same event as her. But she looked so excited to buy it for me. I couldn't graciously decline.

"Thank you," I said, not knowing what else to say. "That's very kind of you."

She hugged me. "Yay! I'm glad you'll be taking it home! It needs to be owned by someone who will appreciate it. And that's you." She pulled her wallet out of her purse. "Let me go talk to Matt about purchasing it. I'll be right back!"

As soon as she left, I whipped around to face Mark. "Is she rich or something?"

Mark shrugged. "I don't know. I never asked."

"How does she make enough as a teaching assistant to pay for that?"

"No idea, but part of the proceeds are being donated to combat climate change, so it's for a good cause."

"I don't feel bad for accepting it." I was excitedly planning where I would hang it in my apartment. I had a few prints framed on my wall, and this canvas would complement them nicely.

"I'm glad," Mark said. "She wouldn't offer it if she couldn't afford it. Besides, Narisha really likes doing things for other people. Giving them gifts, doing things for them. She'd do all your errands for you if you asked, you know. That's just the kind of person she is."

"That's sweet," I said. "I suppose I express my feelings mostly through words and paint."

"Try to look at it as her expressing her affection for you," he said.

"It's just... a lot."

"Yeah, it is, but that's how she is," he said. "But I think it's worth it, especially when she treats you well."

And he would know, wouldn't he? I smiled.

I didn't know how Mark and Narisha could be so cool about it all. On the surface, they really seemed like two friends. Maybe that's what friends-with-benefits were supposed to be like. Far more chill than I was, that's for sure. Maybe my feelings for Mark were the real problem here.

"Soak it up. This is your favourite part, isn't it?" he asked. "The part where you're both falling for each other."

"It is," I affirmed. "I've just never fallen for someone like her before."

"Get ready, then," he said. "She's definitely a challenge."

Before I could ask him exactly what he meant, Narisha appeared by our side again, glowing.

"I got the painting!" she exclaimed.

"That's great!" I said. "Thank you so much!"

"You'll have to invite me over so I can help you hang it up," she said.

There was an expectant look in her eyes. She wanted me to ask her over to my place tonight. This was a clever, albeit expensive, way of doing that.

"I'd love that," I said. "How about we go over there after this and hang it together?"

She lifted her glass of wine. "Deal."

Chapter
SEVEN

The rest of the night flew by. We spent most of it talking with other artists about their work. There were a few shows coming up I absolutely had to attend. Most of them were concept artists, and their paintings were beautiful. One of the artists showed me his work on his phone, and the beautiful sunsets and landscapes were enough to take my breath away. I knew I'd have to see these paintings in person once they were ready for display.

When we were ready to go, Narisha and I said our goodbyes to Mark. They hugged quickly and said bye. Mark and I hugged too, and I felt almost disappointed that we didn't kiss goodbye like we usually did. I had become accustomed to it that its absence felt weird. But it made sense. He probably didn't want to make things harder for me.

Narisha and I took a cab back to my place with the canvas in tow. It had been wrapped so it wouldn't get damaged during the ride home. I wondered if she had planned the whole thing as soon as I had told her that I was visiting the art gallery. That would explain why she had been so determined to find a painting to buy and why she had been so attentive to my favourite ones that evening.

She left her hand on my thigh the entire ride home. I don't know why, but it made my heart race. We had touched before, but having her hand on my leg as she drove was so attractive. When she removed her hand, I was a little disappointed. But not for long. Once we got out of the taxi, she kissed me.

"Thanks for a great evening," I said as I pulled away from her face.

"Oh, the evening's not over yet," she said. "Let's hope you've got some wine up in your apartment because I think we'll need to celebrate more."

"Will we?" I asked, feeling a tingling in my chest. I liked where this was going. "Then let's go!"

We headed inside together. We rushed to my apartment, laughing as I clumsily fidgeted with my purse.

Thankfully, I had kept my apartment relatively clean in the last few days. My painting corner was still a bit messy, but that was okay. It was the one part of my apartment that I let get out of hand. It was part of my process. The rest of my place was clean, though.

I headed to the kitchen and pulled out a bottle of red wine. "Will this do?" I asked.

She gently rested the canvas against the wall. "I think so, yes. Do you already know where you want to put this?"

"On that wall right there," I said, pointing at a blank wall. "It'll liven up the hallway with all the blue tones."

"You're right," she said, accepting a glass of wine I poured for her. "It will."

"Know what else will liven up this place?" I asked.

"What's that?"

"More kisses from you," I said.

She smiled. "That can be arranged."

We sat down on the couch, placing our glasses of wine on the coffee table before us. She kissed me on the cheek, then on the neck. I closed my eyes and enjoyed it.

"I like you a lot," I said.

"That's good," she said. Her hair fell into my face. "Because I like you a lot, too."

"I've honestly been obsessing over you."

"Really?" she asked, playing with my hair. I wished she would do that forever. "Because I've been obsessing over you, too."

I was thrilled to hear that. I beamed and kissed her again, pulling her down toward me.

She paused. "Before we continue, there's something I should mention. I tend to like to be the only one someone is intimate within a day. Does that make sense?"

I moved away from her so I could adjust my sitting position. "That's no problem."

"You're not upset?" she asked.

"Of course not! I'm glad you felt you were able to tell me."

"Thank you," she said.

"I get it," I said and meant it. It would weird me out, too, if she had told me that she had slept with someone else that day. "I hadn't even considered that perspective. I'm still so new to all of this. Sometimes, it's hard for me to know what's wrong and right. For example, I was totally nervous tonight."

"About what?" she asked.

"I didn't know if it would be awkward or not to have you, me, and Mark in the same room. But you were both totally great about it, so I had no reason to worry."

She held my hand. "It's all right. I know it's new to you, and you're still figuring things out. But now you know where I stand with things like that. So, we've grown, in a way."

I smiled. "I like that."

"For me, keeping certain things separate is what keeps the romance alive in my relationships."

"Is it like that for everyone?" I asked.

"No. Everyone has different things they're comfortable with. Everyone can define romance differently. That's just how it is for me."

"Thank you for explaining."

She kissed me. "And thank you for understanding. I know living a poly lifestyle is an adjustment, but we'll work through it together."

That warmed me. She wanted to do it together. "I'm glad to be working through it with you."

"You are?" she asked.

"We worked through this conversation together. I'd say that makes us good teammates."

She laughed. "A teammate? Is that what I am?"

"That's not what I meant. I just meant you were guiding me and doing a good job at it."

"I know," she said. "I'm just teasing you."

I looked at the clock. It was already 11:00 p.m. "Would you like to stay over tonight?"

"Sure. I have work tomorrow, but nobody will notice I didn't change my clothes."

"You can borrow some of mine," I offered.

"That would be great, actually. I think we're around the same size. I'd probably just need to borrow a blouse or something."

"That's no problem," I said. "I'm glad we had another date."

"Did tonight really count as a date?" she asked.

"I consider it a date," I said. "I got to spend time with you and get to know you better." I shrugged. "Sounds like a date to me."

She squeezed my hand. "You make a good point."

"There's one thing we have to do before we go to bed, though," I said.

"What's that?" she asked.

I pointed to the canvas sitting near the door. "We have to hang that up."

"Oh, that's right." She giggled. "That was the whole point of coming over, wasn't it? To help you set that up."

"Except it clearly wasn't your only motivation," I observed.

She smiled. "No, I suppose not."

I stood up and put my hands on my hips. "Let's get it done, then!"

After I assembled all the necessary tools, we placed a stool and worked together to hang the painting up. It looked great on my wall, and it did brighten up the place. The beautiful colours of the mermaid's tail almost sparkled in the lamplight.

Narisha stood back and admired the work. "Wow. It looks great." She turned to me. "Aren't you glad you decided to go to the art gallery after all?"

I smiled. "I am. If I hadn't, I wouldn't be here with you."

"And you wouldn't have this gorgeous piece to add to your collection," she said. "Speaking of your collection, I'd like to see your paintings."

I thought of the painting of Gen. I was *definitely* not showing her that one. Polyamorous or not, she likely did not want to see the last memory I had of my me and my ex in love.

"Maybe another time," I said. "Should we get ready for bed?"

"Sure," she said. "Though I don't have a toothbrush."

"Don't worry, I always keep a spare," I said. "Just in case I bring home a charming woman from an art show."

She rolled her eyes. "Very funny."

We both took turns brushing our teeth. I went first, which meant I was stuck waiting for her in bed. It was nerve-racking to think of Narisha sleeping next to me.

Narisha came out of the bathroom and sat next to me on the sheets. "What's up? You went quiet all of a sudden."

"Well..." I wrung my shirt in my hands. "The truth is, I'm kind of nervous about you sleeping over."

"You're nervous about lots of things, aren't you?" she teased. "First Mark, now this. Don't you know you have nothing to worry about with me? I'm *into* you. That won't change over something as simple as a sleepover."

"But it's not so simple," I said. "I have sleep problems."

She inclined her head. "What kind of sleep problems?"

"I talk in my sleep."

"I'm a heavy sleeper. My roommate practically had a concert in our living room once, and I slept through all of it. And even if you woke me up, I would gently tell you to go back to sleep."

"You wouldn't be freaked out?" I asked.

She shook her head. "Nope. It wouldn't freak me out. It takes way more than that to scare me."

"Okay."

Narisha changed into something more comfortable. She left her clothes by the edge of my bed. I had already seen her in a bathing suit, so her amazing figure was hardly a surprise.

She could have anyone she wanted, but tonight, she had chosen me. She kissed me, her hands trailing down my sides. Then everything slowed down until we were holding hands and gazing at each other from across the bed.

"I think that's all I can do for tonight," Narisha said.

"Next time," I said.

"Promise?"

"I promise."

"Good. Then let's go to sleep."

We both closed our eyes, but I couldn't sleep. My heart was still pounding. I felt elated, excited, and nervous. It was like being a teen again. I feared how much I liked her. I wasn't supposed to fall for people this quickly, not anymore. And yet, here I was, lying in bed freaking out over how much I liked the woman next to me.

After a while, though, exhaustion finally gripped me, and I fell asleep.

When I woke up, Narisha was holding me by the shoulders.

"Hey. Are you awake?" she asked.

I looked around the room. Sunlight wasn't shining through the curtains yet, so I figured it was still nighttime. The second thing I noticed was that I was covered in sweat. Narisha looked really concerned for me.

"What happened?" I asked groggily.

"You were sleep talking," she explained, dropping her hands from my shoulders. "You were crying, too. Saying things like 'Don't leave me' over and over again." She frowned. "Are you okay?"

"Ugh." I buried my face in my hands. "I am so sorry. I really hoped that wouldn't happen tonight. I didn't want you to see me like that. This is mortifying."

"Don't be mortified," she said. "Remember what I told you before we went to bed? That your sleep issue doesn't scare me. And it didn't. I was totally fine. I was just concerned for you. You seemed really upset. Were you having a nightmare?"

I looked up. "Yeah."

The worst part was that I knew exactly what she was talking about. Before she had woken me up, I had been having a nightmare about Gen breaking up with me. I had been having those ever since she left me. I wasn't proud to admit how deeply she had hurt me. And I certainly didn't want to admit it to the girl I was currently infatuated with.

"Do you want to talk about it?" she offered.

I considered saying no. I knew that telling her I still dreamt of my ex would probably be a bad sign. But I also wanted to be honest with her. She had been honest with me earlier that night about her boundaries.

"It was about my ex," I admitted. "Ever since she left me, I've been having horrible nightmares. I've been terrified of being alone."

Narisha winced. "I'm sorry. It sounds like you were really hurt."

"I was," I said. "And I'm getting over it. But when I'm asleep, all those old feelings come back to haunt me."

"That must be tough."

"Does it bother you that I still have nightmares about her?" I asked. "I don't want you to think that makes me less interested in you or something…"

"Of course not!" she exclaimed. "It doesn't bother me that you have nightmares about a difficult ex. I still have nightmares about mine, too, and more than one! And mine weren't all that great either. So, I totally get why you'd be having nightmares about it."

"Do you still want to see me?"

"Yes. Of course. I'm still very much interested in seeing you. I'm just telling you that it might take time for the nightmares to go away. But don't worry about me. If I'm here with you and you have another nightmare in the future, I'll do the exact same thing. I'll wake you up and try to calm you down."

"You're too kind," I said, my eyelids feeling heavy.

"I'm not," she said. "It's what any decent person would do."

"Oh, I don't know," I said. "Most people would be out of here by now. But you're staying by my side." I yawned. "I really appreciate that."

Maybe my mental health issues weren't as big of a barrier as I thought after all. To be fair, she cared about these issues. She studied it in university, after all.

"You're welcome," she replied.

We laid back down together. This time, I felt safe knowing that she was looking out for me. That if anything like this happened again, she would know what to do. And she was good at it, too.

I slept soundly through the rest of the night.

We spent the next month at each other's apartments. Last night, it was my turn to host. Most of our time was spent ordering food in. Narisha's schedule was jam-packed with courses. When she wasn't working on school-related projects, she was spending time with her primary partner. I was glad for the nights we were able to spend together, even if we didn't go out much. It meant more quality time together. This included sleeping in on Saturday mornings.

My phone rang.

"I'll let it go to voicemail," I said, pulling Narisha close. She hummed contentedly and buried her face in my shoulder. Ghost was at the foot of the bed, sleeping near our feet.

We cuddled for the good part of an hour before getting up and getting dressed. I lent her one of my dressy blouses for her class. It was just a white dress shirt, but she made it look great. She had a bad habit of forgetting her clothes at home, but I suspected it was so she could borrow more of mine.

I went to the kitchen to start our breakfast.

"What would you like to eat?" I called to the bathroom where she was putting on her makeup.

"Oatmeal is good," she said.

I opened a couple of bags of oatmeal, and within minutes, our breakfast was ready. I sprinkled a few berries on top for added sweetness.

When she joined me at the table, she looked pristinely put together. Her hair was tied up, and her bronze skin glowed.

"I love raspberries!" She exclaimed as she spotted her breakfast sitting on the table.

"I'm glad," I said, genuinely enjoying her glee over the fruit in her bowl. She was easy to please. "Are you looking forward to work today?"

"Yeah, actually," she said, and her eyes lit up. "The professor is giving a lecture on emotions. It was always my favourite topic when I was an undergrad."

"Why?"

"Because emotions are so complex and diverse," she replied. "And they're not always straightforward."

"That's for sure."

"Maybe you should drop in for a lecture sometime," she said. "I know the professor wouldn't mind. And you might learn something new!"

"Maybe I will," I said. It sounded interesting enough. It was also an excuse to spend more time with her, so I was game.

My phone started ringing again from the bedroom.

"Seems someone wants to get in touch with you," she observed. "They've called twice now."

I went into my room to get my phone. "Let me check who it is."

The caller ID appeared in big, bold letters: Gen.

I groaned. I did not want to have to deal with her right now. Not after having such a nice night with Narisha.

"Who is it?" she asked from the kitchen.

I turned my phone on silent and shoved it in my pocket. "Remember the ex I told you about?"

"Seriously? She's calling you?"

I returned to the kitchen. "Yeah. I don't know what that's about."

"Maybe she's unhappy with your decision to avoid talking to her this past month," Narisha said.

"Probably. But what will calling me accomplish? It will only make things worse."

"When people get desperate, sometimes they act irrationally."

I ran a hand over my face. "I didn't want to have to deal with her this morning."

"And technically, you don't have to. Just because she's calling you doesn't mean you have to answer. But you could always text asking her to leave you alone. That way, you don't have to engage with her, but you'll still make yourself clear."

"True." I sighed. I sat down at the table with Narisha. "I'll do that then."

I took out my phone. I had four missed calls, all from Gen. I opened the messenger app.

> Me: Please stop calling me. I don't feel like talking right now.
> Gen: It's important.

Me: I'm sorry. We'll have to talk later.

"What is she saying?" Narisha asked from the other side of the table.

I took a bite of my oatmeal. "She said it's important, but I told her we're done talking."

"Good for you," Narisha said with a smile. She started eating her breakfast, too. "I know how hard it can be to set boundaries with exes who don't want to leave you alone."

"Do you have experience with that?"

"Oh, yeah," she said. "I had an ex camp outside my door before."

"Did you call the cops?"

"Didn't need to," she said. "But I thought about it."

"That's tough. I'm sorry that happened."

"How are you feeling about her getting back in touch with you?"

"It's kind of intimidating," I said. "Gen is headstrong. If she wants something, she usually gets it through force of will. But this is one thing she won't get from me."

"But you're strong, too," Narisha said. "You can be clear about your needs without giving in to her."

"I know." I took Narisha's hand. "Thanks for listening to me vent about this. I know it's not the most romantic thing to do in the morning."

"Screw romance," Narisha said. "I want real. And this is real life. You're dealing with a problem, and I'm here to help you deal with it."

There was a knock on the door. I frowned. "I'm not expecting anyone."

"Maybe it's a delivery?" Narisha offered.

"I don't remember ordering anything online."

When I opened the door, I was greeted by Gen.

"I've called you like twenty times in a row," Gen said.

"Gen!" I exclaimed, closing the door behind me so she wouldn't see Narisha sitting at the table. "I told you I don't want to talk right now."

"And I told you, it's important," she said. "Why won't you listen?"

"I think you're the one who isn't listening, actually," I shot back. "In what world does 'I don't feel like talking right now' translate into 'Please show up at my apartment'?"

"You weren't picking up your phone, so I didn't have a choice," she said. "I told you it's important, and it is."

"Is this about getting back together? Because I told you..."

"It's not about that," she interrupted. "It's about the cat."

I was stunned. "The cat?"

"Yes. Ghost. I think she belongs with me."

I thought back to Ghost, sitting on the couch purring softly. Gen had never really taken an interest in her, so when we broke up, the cat stayed with me. In fact, Gen hadn't asked for a single update on Ghost since we'd broken up. And now she was saying the cat belonged with her?

"I don't think so," I said. "You've barely checked in with the cat. You certainly haven't come by to visit. I don't think the cat belongs with you. I think she's fine where she is."

"I didn't visit because I was still dealing with the breakup," Gen said. "Now that we've clearly both moved on, I think it's time to take back what's mine."

"Ghost is not yours!" I exclaimed. "I don't know how you can even act like you're entitled to her at all! Who do you think has been taking care of her?"

"And I think it's wonderful you took such good care of her, but now it's time for her to come home with me."

I crossed my arms in front of my chest. "No."

"Isabelle, I'm getting that cat today whether you like it or not."

"Why are you suddenly so interested in Ghost?" I asked. "You haven't asked a thing about her since we broke up. And now you show up on my doorstep demanding I give her to you. Doesn't that seem ridiculous?"

"Don't you dare call me ridiculous," Gen said. "I do not need you to invalidate me like that right now."

I rolled my eyes. It was a typical Gen move. "If you want, you can visit Ghost, but I'm not letting you take her."

"Fine, if you're standing in my way, I'll have to do this."

She pushed past me and threw open the door. She was likely expecting to find an empty apartment because she froze when she saw Narisha sitting at the table. Narisha was sitting there with her legs crossed and a stormy expression.

"Oh, it's you," Gen said with narrowed eyes.

"Yes, it is," Narisha said. "I would say that it's nice to finally meet you, but I think we both know that isn't true."

I stormed in after her. "Get out of my apartment."

"I'm here to take my cat back," Gen said.

"She's not your cat!" I exclaimed. "She's mine. What is this really about?"

Gen spun around to face me. "You want to know what this is *really* about?"

I threw my hands into the air. "Yes!"

"This is really about you choosing some Instagram influencer over me! This is about me offering to fix our relationship and you deciding that it just wasn't good enough for you!"

"That is not how it happened at all, and you know it," I said.

"Then why are you dating a polyamorous person who isn't me? Why wouldn't you try it out with me? Why does it have to be someone new?"

"Because you broke my heart, Gen! You destroyed my trust in you. How many times do I have to tell you that? And rushing into my apartment threatening to steal my cat from me isn't doing you any favours."

"You know, you keep calling her your cat, but I'm pretty sure I was the one who paid for her. In fact, I still have the receipt. So technically, she's my cat."

"But you don't even care about her!" I shouted.

"I care enough to come get her," she said. "So please, go get her carrier, and we'll leave you in peace."

"No."

"I think you should leave," Narisha said, finally breaking her silence. "She clearly doesn't want you here."

"I'm not leaving until I get what I came here for," Gen said.

"Would you like the police to get involved?" Narisha said, holding her phone up to her ear. "Because I have them dialled. I just have to press the call button."

"And what will you tell them? That the rightful owner of a cat is here to pick up her animal and that the babysitter is refusing to give it up? Come on, please. The police would be on my side."

I balled my hands into fists at my sides. "She's right. Don't call the police. They'd probably only side with her."

Narisha looked at me with pleading eyes. "We can't just let her get away with this, though. We have to do something."

"You're going to 'let me get away with it' because you don't have a choice," Gen said. "Now, please. Go get Ghost."

I was trapped. I didn't know what else to do. I found Ghost lounging on my bed. I pet her head gently and kissed her nose. "I'm sorry, baby, but I think you have to go away for a while."

She mewed back at me, and tears sprung to my eyes. I had always loved my pets dearly. I never expected to wake up and have her ripped away from me. But Gen was serious, and she had the paperwork to prove that the cat was legally hers.

I put Ghost into her carrier and brought her out for Gen. I couldn't help the tears streaming down my face. I tried to think of ways I could persuade her to let me keep Ghost, but none of them seemed like they would work.

This was all so petty. Gen was unhappy that I was dating someone other than her, and now she had decided to make my life difficult. I had no doubt that if I told Narisha then and there that I couldn't see her anymore, that Gen would let me keep the cat.

But I wasn't willing to do that. I wasn't willing to give in to her manipulations.

So, I gave her Ghost, my fur baby and my best friend.

"Thank you," Gen said smugly. "That wasn't so hard, was it?"

"It *is* hard," I said, still crying. "This is one of the hardest things you've made me do, and you don't seem to realize how much it hurts me."

"Oh, I realize," Gen said. "And maybe now you'll understand how much you've hurt *me*."

With that, she took Ghost and left.

I collapsed into Narisha's arms afterward. She rubbed my back and hushed me.

"Shh, it's going to be okay," she said over and over while I muffled my sobs in her shoulder.

I felt bad for ruining the shirt she was wearing when she had to go to work, but I couldn't stop the tears. I couldn't believe what Gen had just done. I knew she was spiteful, but I never thought she would barge into my home and take away my cat just because she didn't like that I was dating someone new.

"I never knew Gen could be so petty," I sniffled.

"But now we know," Narisha said. "And we can move forward with that knowledge."

"I don't know what she'll try to do next," I said. "But I can only imagine it's horrible."

"Don't worry about what hasn't happened yet," Narisha said, taking me by the shoulders. "Let's focus on what's happened already and what we can do to fix it."

I wiped my eyes. "Gen took my baby, and I have no idea how to get her back."

"We'll find a way. Even though you didn't pay for her, that is your cat. There must be some way for us to prove that. And when we do, we'll get her back."

I hugged her. "Thank you."

"I'm so sorry to see you getting bullied like this," Narisha said. "It's not right, and I won't stand for it. Not when it's happening to someone as great as you."

"*You're* the great one," I said. "You had to not only deal with me talking in my sleep but also subsequently deal with my ex-girlfriend. Most people wouldn't stick around after that."

She smiled. "I like you. A lot. And these things you think make you unworthy or less worthy of love? They don't matter to me. I don't care that you have nightmares and talk in your sleep. I don't care that you have an ex who won't leave you alone. I'm here for *you*. And I really like you. So that's why I'm still here."

"I appreciate it so much," I said. "I really do."

"I promise to always do my best to be there for you when you need me," she said.

"I hope I can return the favour and be there for you sometime."

"There's plenty of time for that yet." She kissed my forehead. "I have to get to work. But I'll have my phone on me, so you can text me whenever you need me, okay?"

"Okay," I said, a little sad that she had to leave.

"Do you think you'll get much work done today?" she asked.

"Probably not... I foresee a lot of crying over Ghost's things."

She kissed me. "Try not to be too sad, honey. Have faith that it'll all work out."

A few seconds later, she was gone. And I was left alone in my apartment, now emptier than ever before. At least when Gen and I broke up, I had Ghost to keep me company. Now, I had nobody. Just silence.

I texted Alex and told her about what happened. My message ended up looking like a small novel, but I couldn't help it. I became emotional when I was telling her about how Gen burst into my place and stole my cat from me.

I turned on a podcast so it would feel like there were other people around. Then I laid down on the couch with a cold cloth on my face to try and bring down the swelling in my eyes that would surely come after crying so much.

I hoped that Narisha was right and that we'd be able to find help from one of her law school friends. But even with legal help, I would need to find a way to ensure that Gen never tried something like that again. I had to fight back. The only problem was that I wasn't as petty as her. I wouldn't sink to her level. I just hoped there was a way to convince her to leave me alone without having to be spiteful.

Chapter
EIGHT

"I still can't believe she thought it was okay to barge into your apartment," Narisha said. "You did great by setting your boundaries with her."

It had been a few days since our encounter with Gen, and Narisha and I were enjoying a cup of tea together before she headed off for work.

I was worried. I hadn't heard much from Gen since. When we did text, it was to fight. I wished I knew she was treating Ghost well. I didn't think she would be malicious, but I had no way of knowing, and sometimes, my anxiety ran away with thoughts of Ghost being abused.

I had been worried that Narisha would leave after everything that had happened. But she stayed. For the last few days, Narisha had come over after class. We spent most of our time talking, cuddling, and watching movies. Last night we cooked a vegetarian meal together. This morning, we barely ate. Narisha was doing her best to make me comfortable in an unfortunate situation. Though I could never stop worrying about Ghost, she made the anxiety less intense. I was glad to have her around.

"I just hope we can find a way to get Ghost back," I said. "I haven't been able to get anywhere with Gen."

Narisha had been the first to fall asleep the night before, and I had taken out Ghost's little crate of toys. It inspired me to paint my feelings. I painted Ghost as I remembered her: happily curled up, her tail wrapped around her body, and her ears perked up attentively. I had photos of my sweet baby girl, but painting her made me feel closer to her somehow, even though she was far away. I had a piece of her with me that I could look at when I missed her. It didn't bring me much comfort, but it reminded me that I knew her best. I was the one who could paint her from memory, not Gen. I was her rightful owner, and I had to hope that we would be reunited soon.

"Just don't answer if she texts you, all right? Only answer if she offers to let you see Ghost," Narisha said. "Hopefully, she got the message and will leave you alone now."

I nodded. "Hopefully."

She hugged me tightly. "I'll be thinking of you today."

"Me, too."

"Bye!"

After a few minutes, I checked my phone. Narisha had already sent me a message.

> Narisha: Thinking of you, babe! Hope you're doing okay. Why don't we plan a nice soothing afternoon for you sometime soon to make up for all of this?

I didn't deserve her. And yet, there she was. And I couldn't help but admit that I liked it when she called me "babe." The fact that she was already calling me pet names seemed promising.

> Me: It really means so much that you've been supporting me.

Narisha: Of course :)

My phone rang. A jolt of fear hit me in the chest. I was worried that it was Gen calling again to harass me. But this time, it wasn't an ex. It was Alex.

"Alex," I said as I picked up. "I'm glad it's you."

"I just read your texts about Gen," she said. "Sorry, I'm a few days behind on my messages. Are you okay?"

"I'm really sad, to be honest. I can't believe she took my baby from me. Poor Ghost."

"Why don't I come over and see you?"

"You don't have to come over. I was going to get some work done eventually, anyway. I just needed a breather..."

"Nonsense. You need more than a breather." I could hear her blinker clicking. She was already driving over. "I'm off work today. And we both know that you're probably not going to get any work done right now. I can hear that groggy tone. So, I'm coming over to hang out."

I smiled. "Even though I didn't invite you over."

"That's what best friends are for," she said. "They're there for you even when you don't ask them to be."

"Thanks, Alex. I appreciate it."

"So, is Ghost really gone?"

"Yeah." I sighed. "She took her. I don't know what to do."

"Gen really broke into your place?"

"She didn't break in." I sighed. "She took her things. She was a bit forceful about it, though."

"God. What a mess."

"Nobody was hurt. Not physically, anyway."

"I can't believe her." There was a pause. "Look, I'm almost at your place. I'll see you soon?"

"Okay. See you soon."

I got up, made the bed, and tidied up the apartment. Thankfully, it was still relatively clean from the night before. I only had to do the dishes from the breakfast we made.

"Hi," I said, fighting back tears when I opened the door.

"Hey!" Alex replied.

I hugged her. "Thanks for coming over."

"Don't mention it."

I stepped back. "Would you like some tea?"

"Sure!" she said.

I set the kettle to boil. Within a few minutes, our chai was steeping nicely in our mugs. I sat next to her on the couch.

"I'm so sorry about everything that's happened with Ghost," Alex said.

I wiped my eyes. "I know. It's terrible."

"Do you know how you're going to get her back? If I were you, I'd probably be breaking down her door right about now."

"I want to, believe me," I said. "But I know she'll be petty and likely call the police on me for breaking and entering. I'm not going to do that. But I desperately want Ghost back."

"Of course you do," Alex said. "She's your baby, after all. Didn't you get her when she was little?"

"Yeah." It broke my heart to think of Ghost, fluffy and white, in the palm of my hand as a kitten. She had grown several times the size, but now she was nowhere in sight. "I don't know how I'm going to manage without her. I painted her last night because I missed her so much."

I got up and pulled out the painting I had done of Ghost.

"Awww," Alex said. "It looks just like her. You did a great job."

"Thank you." I sat back down. "I wish she was here."

"I know you'll figure this out. You'll get her back."

"I hope so."

"I'd say it's only a matter of time before she's back home. You're the rightful owner, and anyone who knows you and Ghost can attest to that. You even have proof that Gen didn't check up on Ghost at all while you were broken up."

"Yeah. And when we were together, she barely took care of Ghost at all," I said. "Sometimes she'd play with her, but that's about it. She didn't take her to the vet or buy her special food and medication when she was sick. I did."

"You did, and any reasonable lawyer or whatever would recognize that," Alex said. "I hope it doesn't have to go that far for your sake, obviously. But if it does, I think the law is on your side."

"She argued because she had purchase receipts that Ghost belonged to her," I said. "There has to be more to ownership than that, though!"

"I'd say," Alex agreed. "She had no right coming in here uninvited and pressuring you into giving her your pet. That's just not right. I have half a mind to give her a visit, myself."

"Alex, don't," I said. "I'll keep trying to get her to let me visit or send picture updates or something. I'll wait a little while before actually showing up at her apartment."

"Why? Are you scared she'll do something?"

"I just don't want Ghost to get hurt in all of this," I said. "I hope she's safe with Gen, but given how unpredictable she's been lately, it's hard to say what she'll do next."

"I'll be here for you through thick and thin," Alex said.

I hugged her. "Thank you so much for talking this out with me."

"Anytime."

I sipped my tea. "Let's talk about lighter things."

"Sure. Whatever will help." Alex motioned to the new painting hanging up on the wall. "I noticed you have a new piece added to your collection."

"Oh, yeah. That's Narisha's doing. She bought me that painting at the gallery."

"Are you kidding?" Alex said. "It's so big. You must be happy with it."

"I am." I smiled. "But I wasn't the one who picked it out. Narisha has an eye for art."

"Wow. It's nice to see your face light up when you talk about her."

"Do I? I haven't noticed."

Alex took a sip from her tea. I had put two milk and one sugar in hers. I didn't like sugar, but Alex always took her tea the same. "And how did she deal with Gen coming over like that?"

"She dealt with it really well, actually," I said. "If I was in her position, I'd be so out."

"I know what you mean. If I was dating a girl and her ex showed up in the morning screaming, I'd probably have second thoughts."

My stomach sank. "I really hope she doesn't do that. I like her too much."

"I don't think she will," Alex said, patting me on the shoulder. "She's been texting you this whole time, right?"

I checked my phone. I had three unread messages, all from her. "You're right. She's not going to stop seeing me because of Gen. She's being totally understanding about it all."

"She really is," Alex said. "I'm impressed with her. She knows that the actions of your ex don't reflect on you."

"Yeah. But I wouldn't blame her if she decided she didn't want to deal with the drama."

"We'll leave that up to her to decide."

I sipped my own tea. "True. The choice is hers to make, not mine."

"Emotions run wild in polyamory," Alex said. "There's bound to be some drama. People are going to clash. Not everyone is going to agree or get along. Narisha's been polyamorous for a few years."

"That's true," I said, feeling a bit relieved.

"So how have things been, otherwise?" Alex asked. "You've been getting out more, which I like."

"Yes, I have," I said. "And believe it or not, I like it too."

"Wow. Proud extrovert moment."

I laughed. "Things have been going really well lately."

"I imagine you've been enjoying the romance of it all," she said.

I thought for a moment. "Yeah, I guess things have been romantic. Narisha and I cuddled all night. It felt really intimate. We don't always have time for sleepovers, but I'm grateful for when we do."

"That's great! So, there was some progress there, at least," she said.

"Yeah. We've been spending as much time together as we can."

My phone buzzed. Another text message.

Alex pointed to it. "You can answer that. I'll check my messages, too."

"Okay," I said.

The first three messages were from Narisha. The last one piqued my interest.

> Narisha: Hey. Eliza is going to be back home in two days. Would you be interested in meeting her?

Alex nudged me with her elbow. "What did she say?"

I showed her the text. "She wants me to meet her primary partner."

"Oh." Alex looked up from the text to me. "How do you feel about that?"

"I don't know," I said. "She only just texted me. I haven't really had time to think about it."

"I mean, you were nervous about going to the art gallery because both Mark and Narisha were there," Alex said. "But in the end, there was no reason to be nervous. They were totally cool with each other."

"I know, but Eliza isn't Mark. Narisha's relationship with him is super casual. Her relationship with Eliza is super not."

"Does that mean you don't want to meet with her?" she asked.

"No, I do, it's just..." I chewed on my bottom lip. "It's a big deal, isn't it?"

"Yeah, it is," Alex replied. "She's asking you to meet the most important person in her life. That's my understanding of what a primary partner is."

"I think it's whoever is highest in the relationship hierarchy," I said. "Though I could be wrong."

"I think it could be both," Alex said. "This is great news, though. The fact that she wants you to meet means you must've made a good impression."

"I hope you're right."

"Will it be uncomfortable for you to meet someone she's in a serious relationship with?" Alex asked. "I don't know about you, but I'd feel pretty insecure."

"I haven't even agreed to meet her yet, and I'm already intimidated," I said. "But it could also be great. If her primary partner approves of me, that could win me points with Narisha."

"Do you really think that's how it works? If the other person likes you, you'll have an easier time in the relationship?" Alex asked.

"I don't know much about polyamory, but I think it would work best if everyone got along. Don't you?"

"True. So, what will you do?"

"I'll meet with them." I tried to ignore my trembling fingers. "It'll be nerve-racking, but I think it'll be helpful in the long run. Especially if I want to keep seeing Narisha."

"Are you jealous at all? That she has a primary partner?"

"To be honest, I might feel a little envious of their time together," I said. "But that's probably just my old monogamous ways coming out. I think I'm more comfortable with monogamy because that's all I've known. But I like Narisha. Part of dating her means meeting Eliza. I'm okay with that."

"How much time do they spend together, usually? Does that leave enough time for you?"

"They spend the weekends together, typically," I said. "That's when Eliza is off work and not totally exhausted from her day job."

"Does it bother you that you don't get to spend weekends together?"

"It depends," I said. "I get lots of time with her during the week, and like I said, she stays over. So, I get to sleep next to her."

"But that's not exactly the same as spending time together awake, right?"

"Yeah. I guess you're right. It is a little different when most of our time together is spent sleeping. If we had weekends together, too, we could go out more and do stuff."

"Do you envy Eliza for being able to go out and do all that stuff with her?"

"Well, Narisha really likes going to the beach," I said. "She also likes hikes. I know I'm not much of an outdoorsy person. So, I'm glad she has someone she can do those things with. But I also won't have the opportunity to try and do them with her because our dates are reserved for evenings after she's done class."

"Basically, you wish you at least had the chance to go out with her, yeah?"

I nodded. "I might not be the sportiest person, as you know, but I like trying new things now and then. And I'd like to try new things with her, too."

"Maybe that's something you could bring up when you're all together," Alex suggested.

I swallowed hard. "I don't know. I think that could lead to a conflict, and I want to avoid one. I want Eliza to like me. I don't want to walk into our first meeting making demands on their shared time together."

"Wow." Alex exhaled deeply. "I just realized you're stronger than me."

"How so?"

"I wouldn't be able to do what you're doing. I'd be going out of my mind with jealousy, knowing that the person I liked was in love with someone else. I suppose I prefer to be the only person my partner likes. And the scheduling sounds tough to deal with."

"And I can understand why you'd feel that way," I said. "It was how I thought I'd feel up until this point. I mean, I've been monogamous my whole life. But now that I've opened my mind to polyamory, I'm set on seeing it through. I want to experience everything. And that means dealing with... what was it called again? Dealing with my metamours."

"Metamours?"

"It means my partner's partner."

"Oh, right." She took another swig of her tea. "If you think that meeting with Eliza will enhance your relationship with Narisha, then I say go for it. It's clear to me that you're already head over heels for this girl."

I laughed. "I'm not head over heels for her. That's an exaggeration."

"Oh, you most certainly are. You smile when you talk about her. That's how I know you're into her. Even when life is hitting you hard, she still makes you happy."

"You don't know what you're talking about."

"Do so," Alex said. "But what matters is how you feel."

I ran a hand through my hair. "Okay, maybe I *do* like her a lot. But that's why this meeting with her girlfriend is so important. I really want it to go well."

"I think it will. If Narisha is half as good as you make her out to be, she probably has good taste. I mean, she's dating you, so that's saying something."

"Thanks, Alex."

"I've got to go. Nina needs me to drive her to an appointment. But I'm just a phone call away if you need me. You know that, right?"

"I know. Thanks. I really do appreciate you coming over today."

She hugged me tightly. "You're welcome. And stay strong. We'll get your kitty back."

Once Alex was gone, I texted Narisha back.

> Me: I'd love to meet with you and Eliza! When and where were you thinking?
> Narisha: I was thinking we could meet for bubble tea.

Bubble tea seemed like a casual setting. But maybe her girlfriend, Eliza, was really laid back. I had never met her, so it was impossible to say.

> Me: Sounds great to me :) I'm looking forward to meeting her! You're so great, so I imagine she must be great, too.

Narisha: You're too kind. She's looking
forward to meeting you, too! I may have been
talking about you nonstop for the last few
days...

Had she been thinking about *me* nonstop for the last few days? That was my line!

I knew then I had to paint her.

And that's when I knew I really *had* fallen for her, just like Alex said.

Chapter
NINE

The painting would be a portrait of Narisha viewed from above in a blue gown.

Narisha's curls were a challenge for me to paint, even though they were loose. I didn't often paint curls, but hers were so pretty that I knew I had to spend extra time learning how to get them just right. I loved her hair. There was so much to run my fingers through. I tried to capture how soft it was on the canvas.

Painting was a good distraction from the waves of guilt and anxiety I felt crashing over me each time I looked around the apartment to see Ghost was gone. Gen had finally sent me an update with photos of Ghost, letting me know she was okay. But Gen wasn't willing to let me come over and visit her yet. This was the longest I had gone without seeing my baby, and I desperately needed to throw myself into painting to distract myself.

I painted Narisha looking up toward the viewer, her smoky eyeshadow scintillating above her eyes. Her expression was coy, just as I remembered it. I placed her hands on her hips, as though she were issuing a challenge. "Come and get me," her expression said. She looked fierce, and I loved it. It represented her true spirit. Narisha didn't bow down to anyone.

The colours popped vividly. The blue of her gown against the black backdrop drew the eye toward the focal point of the piece. I was elated with how I captured her expression. It was both playful and confident. This was different from my usual work, as I didn't often paint subjects who looked out toward the viewer. It felt like I was doing her justice.

The painting was nowhere near finished, but I had done enough for the day. I took a picture of it to keep for the process. I liked to have photos of each stage of my paintings, from the initial sketch to the final product. I liked posting those images to show people how hard I worked to achieve my goals.

Despite how well the painting was progressing, I was worried about the meeting with Narisha's primary partner. I was meeting with them later this afternoon. I had no idea what to expect. I had managed to find her Instagram account by flipping through Narisha's pictures until I found one of them together. They were on the beach and had their arms wrapped around each other, broad smiles on their faces. They were sun-kissed and in love, it seemed.

For a moment, I felt a flash of jealousy. I didn't like seeing Narisha's arm lovingly wrapped around someone else. I preferred it when her arm was around me. But I realized that just because she posed for pictures with Eliza didn't mean she couldn't pose for pictures with me, too. My jealousy seemed a little irrational. The whole point of polyamory was to share, wasn't it? I was all right sharing her with Mark. But trying out the polyamorous lifestyle meant that I had to be okay with sharing her with Eliza, too.

My biggest problem with the whole Eliza situation was that I didn't know her. I was worried that she was a threat to me. What if she didn't like me? Would she tell Narisha to stop dating me? Narisha seemed to like me, and she said Eliza had asked about me. That meant she was interested in me and would probably be friendly. But I had never experienced anything like this, so it was hard to know how it would turn out. I hoped for the best.

My thoughts were interrupted by a text from Mark.

```
Mark: I'm here :)
```

We had arranged a short meeting this morning to catch up. That was what we said it was for, but in reality, Mark was visiting to help me calm down in preparation for my meeting with Narisha and Eliza.

When he walked in the door, he had two cupcakes in his hands. "I bring gifts!"

"Oh, wow!" I exclaimed. "Those look delicious. What kind are they?"

"Red velvet," he said. "I thought you might need a little pick-me-up."

I kissed him on the cheek. "Thank you so much! I certainly won't say no."

We sat down on the couch together. Mark was wearing dark blue jeans with a tight-fitting black top. I like how he smelled. It was a new scent for him: not sandalwood but pine, as though he had been outside all day.

"So, how nervous are you?" he asked, taking a bite off the top of his cupcake.

"I'm pretty nervous," I said, peeling the wrapper off mine. "I don't know what to expect."

"Don't worry too much about Eliza," Mark said. "She can be a little all over the place, but she means well."

"Wait, you've met her before?"

"Of course," he said. "I've known Narisha for two years now. You think I wouldn't bump into her primary?"

"I just didn't think there'd be a reason for you two to meet," I said. "Given that you're a more casual partner for her."

"Eliza likes to meet all of Narisha's partners, even the casual ones," Mark explained.

"You must've had a similar meeting, then," I said.

"Pretty much, yeah. We went for coffee. It was fine. I think Eliza was a bit nervous, but by the end of it, she was comfortable with me."

"Why do you think she was nervous? I mean, she's already Narisha's primary. It's not like she's the one being interviewed."

He laughed. "Is that how you see it? As an interview?"

I threw up my hands. "How else should I see it? Two people are inviting me out to, like, evaluate me or something. And if I pass, Eliza gives me her approval, and Narisha and I can continue dating. That's what's happening, isn't it?"

Mark pressed a hand to his chin. "I see where you're coming from. I just wouldn't put it like that."

"But that's why this whole thing is so stressful. I feel like if I don't behave well enough, Eliza won't approve of me, and I won't get to see Narisha again."

"Don't worry," Mark said. "If I was able to impress her, I'm sure you won't have a problem."

"Thanks," I said. "I'm glad you shared that with me. I feel a bit more relaxed knowing that it went well for you."

"It'll probably go really well for you, too," he said. "Especially since Narisha likes you so much."

"I hope so!"

"You've barely touched your cupcake," Mark pointed out. His was already completely gone.

"I eat slowly," I said.

"That's not it. I can tell when you're lying."

I hated how well Mark knew me. It meant that I couldn't get away with lying anymore. "I'm still sad. About Ghost."

"I'm sorry," he said. "I can't believe that your ex just took her from you. Have you heard anything from her since?"

"I sent her numerous receipt scans and vet bills to prove that I've been the one taking care of Ghost this entire time and that I'm her legal owner."

"Did she respond?" he asked.

"She told me that Ghost was fine and that I shouldn't worry about her. She said she isn't mistreating her. She sent me some photos. Which is great if I could trust her, but I can't. I have no idea if she's telling the truth or not."

"Yeah, that sucks," Mark said. "I wouldn't trust her at this point, either."

"I shouldn't have trusted her at all!" I exclaimed. "I feel like an idiot for trusting her for even a minute."

"Don't be so hard on yourself," Mark said. "Until this last month, you were still madly in love with her. Of course you're going to be blinded by that."

"I knew she was upset that I wouldn't date her, but I had no idea she would sink to this level," I said.

"Yeah, it seems like it came out of nowhere."

"It did. She tried calling me before she showed up. I almost wish I had answered my phone the first time she called to avoid that disaster."

"You don't know if answering the phone would've stopped her from coming over," he pointed out. "She may have still come over. Taking Ghost was probably her plan all along. To get back at you."

I felt like I was choking. "I'm just worried I won't get her back."

"You will." he smiled comfortingly. "Did Gen say anything else?"

"She told me that if I want Ghost back, I'll have to show her more than receipts."

"So, it didn't work, then."

"No, not really." I sighed. "There must be some other way to convince Gen to give her back without getting the police involved."

"I think that's understandable. But Gen might not respond to anything else."

"I have to try it my way first," I said. "And… if it doesn't work, then yes, I'll go to the police. Though I hope they'll take my side, even after they see both our receipts. Gen says she has ownership because she purchased her."

"God, it's so messed up that she's doing this to you," he said. "I mean, I'd understand if she took care of the cat, too. But she didn't. In fact, I don't think she's ever even posted a selfie with Ghost to social media once. Not that posting pictures is how I evaluate love, but still. People love taking selfies with their pets."

"Not her," I muttered. "She didn't care about Ghost until it was convenient for her."

"I'm sorry," he said. "I know it must suck to have that stress on your shoulders in addition to the stress you're feeling about meeting Eliza."

"I'm going to try and go to the meeting with a positive outlook. I want it to go well."

"I know you do," he said with a smile. "It's pretty cute, actually."

"Cute?" I repeated. "How?"

"I've never seen you with a crush like this," he said. "I've only ever seen you heartbroken. It's a nice change of pace."

I smiled. "Yeah. It is a nice change of pace. I like it, too."

"I hope to see you happy more and more," he said. "And… I hope I'm not being selfish, but I hope I can keep making you happy, too."

"What do you mean?" I asked.

He brushed my hair behind my ear. "I mean, I hope we can continue seeing each other."

"Oh." Things had been so busy with Narisha and preparing to meet Eliza that I hadn't considered his needs fully. I tried to be present and consider what my relationship with her would mean for my future with him. "You want to keep seeing me?"

"Of course I want to keep seeing you." He smiled. "Why wouldn't I?"

I laughed. "I guess I just assumed one of us would have to stop seeing you."

"And why would it be you?" he asked, meeting my eyes. "Narisha has a primary. You don't. Plus, she's made it clear how casual our relationship is."

"You say it like it's a bad thing."

"I'm disposable to her," he said. He laughed, but it wasn't a happy sound. "I know I don't really do romantic relationships, but it still stings a little."

"Why would you say that you're disposable?" I asked. "I've seen you two together. You seem to get along great. I think Narisha really likes you, Mark. You're a good friend to her."

"But as a lover, I'm replaceable," he said. "I'm nothing special to her. I knew that from the beginning. But I have to admit, after a while, it starts to hurt."

I had to stop myself from gaping. Was Mark actually admitting he had *feelings* for someone? He hadn't said he liked Narisha. He just said he didn't like that she didn't hold him up as high as everyone else.

"Are you jealous?" I asked, unable to keep the shock out of my voice.

"I wouldn't say that. I'd just say I wish I meant more to her," he said. "I like to think that each connection I have with someone is special. That it's meaningful, even if it's not romantic. Does that make sense?"

"Honestly, I don't totally get it," I said. "I know you said you don't do romantic relationships, but you must feel some kind of romantic emotion if you're getting jealous."

He shrugged. "I'm human. Sometimes I feel things, it's true. But I try not to let them get to me."

My heart pounded. "Did you ever feel anything like that between us?"

"Between us?" he repeated. "No. But I never had reason to. You've always treated our time together like it was meaningful."

"Because it *is* meaningful to me." I paused. "Maybe more meaningful than it is to you."

"Why would you say that?" Mark asked.

This was the moment where I needed to decide if I wanted to be honest with Mark or keep my feelings for him secret. I knew that if I told him about how I felt, he would likely reject me. He'd made it clear a thousand times that he didn't do romantic relationships. But I had also seen a glimpse of emotion in him. That meant there was potential for more. Possibly with me.

"Because I like you," I confessed. "Romantically. And I know that's not something you do. I understand that. But I can't help the way I feel. I tried to stop it at first. But it didn't work. I just kept developing feelings for you. Every time I came over, it killed me that I had all these feelings for you that I knew weren't returned."

"How can you be so sure I didn't return them?" he asked, crossing his arms in front of his chest.

"Because you always say, 'I don't do relationships.'"

"I don't," he said. He drew closer. "But that doesn't mean I don't have feelings."

"For me?" I asked.

"For you," he replied.

His gaze was piercing.

"I had no idea," I said.

"I didn't really hint at it," he said.

"So, you have feelings for me, but you don't want to have a relationship?"

"Kind of."

I frowned. "I don't understand."

"I just don't like the triviality of relationships. I don't like living with people. I'm not really someone that would ever be a domestic partner, you know? But that doesn't mean I can't have my own kind of relationships with people."

"Essentially nothing between us would change," I said.

"Except for now, we know how we feel."

"But what does it matter how we feel if we're not actually dating?" I asked. "I don't mean to be rude or anything, but I just don't get it. I'm not certain that changes much for me. I thought if I could make you like me, you might change your mind about the whole 'no relationship' thing."

"It's who I am," he said. "But doesn't it make you at least a little happy that I feel the same way about you?"

"I think we just view these things differently."

"We might," he said. "But we can make it work. We've made it work so far."

"I worry that I like you a lot more than you like me. That I'll always like you more than you like me. I can't bear to keep seeing you if I'll always like you more. What happens when I fall in love with you, Mark? Do I hold all of that inside because I know you can't return those feelings?"

"No," he muttered. "That wouldn't be fair."

"It wouldn't," I agreed.

"But I might fall in love with you, too, you know," he said.

"I don't think so," I said.

"How do you know unless you take a chance?" he asked.

His expression looked pained. I felt sorry for him. I didn't want to cause him distress. But I also couldn't understand how our lifestyles could be compatible. I wanted a real relationship, not just something casual with him.

"How would things be different for you?" I asked. "We'd essentially keep doing what we're doing now with no changes. But for me, everything would change. Knowing you feel the same way as I do means I would want more from you."

"What, like meeting your friends?"

"Sure! Or staying over for several days in a row. Or eating breakfast together. Or cuddling. Or calling each other pet names. All that stuff. All the pieces of falling in love. That's what I enjoy most about dating. I honestly don't see the point if romance is out of the picture."

"If that's what you want, we can work it out," he said. "Would it make you happy to do those things with me, too?"

"As opposed to just with Narisha?" I asked.

"Yeah."

"Of course. I might be new to polyamory, but I know I want to do all the coupley things with both of you. I'd like to think each relationship I have is different and meaningful."

"You're right," he said. "I'm sorry. I know relationships aren't just meant to serve one purpose. I guess I've just been hooking up with people for so long that I forgot what dating feels like."

"It's okay," I said. "We've both been going through a lot of changes lately in terms of relationships."

"We have, yeah."

"How about we put this conversation away for another time? It's not that I don't think this is extremely important, because it is. But I still have that meeting with Eliza and Narisha coming up. I don't want to be overwhelmed when I show up."

"Don't worry, I get it," he said. "We'll table it."

"But I'm glad you feel the same way about me," I said and kissed him.

He kissed me back. For a moment, I forgot all of my nerves surrounding the meeting with Eliza. I could only think about how happy I was that Mark had finally admitted he liked me back. Ever since I realized I had feelings for him, it had felt like something was missing between us. Now, I felt like we were closer. And all it had taken was a simple conversation.

"What time is it?" he asked. "I don't want to be the reason you're late."

"With kisses that good, I almost wouldn't mind," I said.

Mark checked his phone. "It's 4:00. Aren't you meeting with them soon?"

"Shit. Yeah. I've gotta run."

"Don't worry about it," he said with a crooked smile. "I think we had a productive chat."

"Me too," I said. "And I look forward to talking more. But right now, I need to brush my teeth and make sure I get there on time. Thank you for stopping by. You really did help ease my nerves about meeting with them."

"You're welcome." He hugged me. "Let me know how it goes, okay?"

"I will."

On the drive to the bubble tea shop to meet with Narisha and Eliza, I was a nervous wreck. I kept imagining that I'd say something wrong. There was so much I didn't know about polyamory. What if I said something offensive without realizing it? What if Eliza disliked me enough that she forbade Narisha from ever seeing me again? I was sweating profusely enough that my hands were slipping on the steering wheel. Thankfully, I managed to park without incident.

I walked into the shop. The walls were painted burgundy, the seats looked cushioned and comfortable, and there was pop music playing. There weren't many people in the store, with only a couple of people chatting and sipping drinks.

I expected to find Eliza and Narisha waiting for me. Instead, I spotted Narisha alone at a table. She waved me over, and I joined her. There were two lidded cups with straws sitting on the table.

"Hey!" I said.

She greeted me with a smile. "Hey. I bought you a drink. I hope you don't mind what I chose for you."

"I don't mind. What kind did you get?"

"Brown sugar tea, I think it's called," she said. "Do you like those?"

"Love 'em'." I took a sip. "Mmm. That tastes great! Why have I never come here before?"

"Guess you just needed to meet the right person," Narisha said.

"I guess you're right," I said. "So, where's Eliza?"

"She had a meeting before this, and it's running a little long," she said. "I told her you probably wouldn't mind the time alone with me."

"True. I would never complain about spending more time with you." I blew out a big breath. "To be honest, I was practically having a mental breakdown in the car."

"A mental breakdown? Why? Did Gen do something again?"

"No, not over Gen. Over this meeting."

"You're that worried about meeting Eliza?" she asked.

"Mark told me he had a similar meeting with you and Eliza, and it went well. That comforted me for a while, but I eventually started panicking again."

Narisha placed her hand on mine. "Deep breaths. It's all going to be okay."

I took a few deep breaths and smiled. "Okay, I'm good."

"You really have no reason to worry so much," Narisha assured me. "We're just hanging out today so you two can get to know each other."

"It doesn't feel like we're hanging out to me. I think it's because she's your primary. I feel like I'm going for a job interview."

"Please don't look at it that way. She just wants to get to know you. And I feel it's important for my partners to meet."

"Why do you feel it's important for your partners to meet?" I asked.

"I see it as building a family."

"Like polygamy?"

She laughed. "No, not like that. I'm polyamorous, not polygamist. I'm not going to marry a bunch of women and make them subservient to me."

"No, that doesn't seem like you," I teased.

"I feel like everyone is connected through each other and that if we make the best of it, it can be like a family."

"Like living together and everything?"

"Not necessarily," she said. "But I wouldn't be totally opposed to the idea." I must've gaped because she said, "Don't worry. Not any time soon."

"Sorry, I've just never considered a life like that," I said, recovering. "Is that something you want?"

"I don't know," she said. "I think it'd be nice to live comfortably with multiple partners. I mean, if you're in love with all of them and dating, why not just live with each other?"

"I imagine there might be friction between partners," I said.

"There could be. But all roommates have a bit of friction, don't they?"

I laughed. "So, would everyone date each other?"

"In my vision, we all live communally together." She shrugged. "It's just a fantasy of mine, anyway. It's not something you need to worry about right now. I promise you, that's not the reason I brought you here today."

"But it is because you want to create a sense of family," I said.

"Yes," she replied. "I want everyone to at least be friendly with each other because, like it or not, we're all connected. My relationship with Eliza will inevitably be affected by my relationship with you."

"Your 'relationship' with me?" I repeated. "I didn't realize we were calling it that already."

She smiled. "You know what I meant."

"I know, I'm just teasing you."

"You seem to be in a better mood today," she said. "How are you holding up?"

"Better, thanks to you and Mark. I've been socializing a lot more."

"I'm glad to hear it," she said. "Oh! There's Eliza now."

I turned around to look at the woman entering the store. She had long blonde hair and was dressed in a black pantsuit with a white dress shirt underneath. Not exactly a comfortable outfit for a laidback hangout at a bubble tea shop. But Narisha had said she had just come from a meeting, so her outfit made sense. Her cheeks were red, as if she had jogged here. She waved at us and then went to the counter to put in an order.

Once Eliza had her tea, she joined us at the table and extended her hand to me. "You must be Bells. Nice to meet you."

"Nice to meet you, too," I said, shaking her hand. She had a firm handshake.

Eliza sighed and fell back into her chair. "God. What a busy day I've had."

"Hopefully, now you can relax," Narisha said.

"I hope so," Eliza said. "Or I might faint on the spot."

"I'm sorry you're feeling so tired," I said.

"Oh, it's fine." She sat up. "It's just end-of-the-day exhaustion."

I figured this whole thing would be easier if I started asking the questions. Plus, then the focus wouldn't entirely be on me.

"What do you do for work?" I asked.

"I'm a human resources manager for a university," she replied.

My eyes widened. "Oh, wow. You must work hard."

"I do," she says.

That's when I noticed the age difference between Eliza and Narisha. Eliza had a young face, but I realized now that she must have been in her early forties. The age difference was more noticeable now that I had them sitting right in front of me. When I was looking at their photos together, I never noticed it. She presented herself confidently, which made all of this ten times more intimidating.

I didn't know what to say. I couldn't bring up how Narisha and I met because she likely already knew that story. I considered telling her about Mark, but I felt it was probably too soon to be talking about him like an official partner.

Eliza took off her jacket and laid it on the back of her chair. "I believe Narisha told me that you're a painter?"

"I am," I said. I was glad she took the initiative in the conversation. "I mostly paint with oils."

"Have you been working on anything new recently?" she asked.

I dropped my gaze to my lap. "Well... I was going to wait to mention this, but I've actually started a painting of Narisha."

"You did?" Narisha exclaimed. "That's incredible!"

I met her eyes. She looked thrilled. "I'm glad you think so."

"Are you basing it off an image of me? Like a reference photo?" Narisha asked.

"No, I'm painting from memory," I said. I could feel the blush creeping up my neck. "I'm using your stunning outfit for the gala as inspiration."

"Oh, so it'll be fancy!" Narisha beamed. "That's perfect."

"What a kind gift," Eliza said. "I look forward to seeing it."

Everyone was smiling, and the conversation was pleasant. Sure, I was a bit intimidated by Eliza, but once she started talking, she seemed like a normal person.

"Narisha also told me that this was your first time dating a polyamorous person," Eliza noted. "How do you find it so far?"

"I don't know if I can say how I find it since I haven't been doing it for long," I said. "It's difficult to give an opinion on anything right now because I've seen how quickly I can change my mind."

"Do you find it enjoyable?" Eliza asked. "Or is it overwhelming for you?"

"It's a little overwhelming, I'll admit," I said. "I've never been in a situation where I had freedom like this before."

"That's understandable. I think everyone is a bit overwhelmed at first."

"When you two started dating, was it difficult?" I asked. "Or were you both on the same page regarding polyamory?"

"It took a lot of talking before we were comfortable with our relationship," Narisha said carefully.

I realized that perhaps I had asked the wrong question. Eliza's lips sloped downward as though she were remembering a fight they had had. "We weren't in agreement at first about what our relationship should look like," Eliza said. "I was monogamous and had always been, so the fact that Narisha wanted to see other people was... hard for me. But we worked on it together until I was comfortable with everything."

"I'm grateful that Narisha is so patient," I said.

"We're both very fortunate to have her in our lives," Eliza said. "And I'm glad we could meet together like this today."

"Me too," I said. "I was worried I'd make a bad impression."

"No way!" Eliza said. "You've made a great impression. Besides, I already knew how well things were going between you two. I had a good feeling about you."

"So does this mean I pass the test?" I asked.

Eliza laughed. "You pass!"

I smiled. "Nice."

Even though things were going so well, my stomach was still in knots. Smaller ones than before, but knots nonetheless. Eliza wrapped an arm around Narisha's shoulders, and the warmth in Narisha's eyes when she glanced at her was enough to make me jealous. I tried to force the feeling down and ignore it, but it was hard.

"It would be nice to do this again," Narisha said. "What do you think?"

"I think that sounds wonderful," I said.

I worried about the tightening feeling in my chest. I wondered if it was a sign that all of this was too much for me. But I didn't want to back down—not yet. Not when things were going so well with Eliza and Narisha. Meeting them for tea was the first step. Learning how to manage my feelings was the next.

Chapter
TEN

The next time Narisha and I were at my place was a few days later. When we walked through my door, she gasped. The canvas I had been working on was on full display in the middle of the living room. I had cleared the coffee table, so I had more space to paint. I regretted that decision now because I had put it exactly where she could see it. I usually didn't like to show the people I loved the paintings I made of them, let alone pieces that weren't done yet. But Narisha didn't seem to mind in the slightest.

"Wow, that's amazing!" she exclaimed. She ran over to the canvas to inspect it. "It looks just like me! Or like a better version of me."

My face burned. "I painted you exactly as I see you."

"And you see me as some kind of *Bridgerton*-esque lady?" she asked.

"I see you as the beautiful woman you are," I said.

"I can't believe it. It's gorgeous." She inspected it further. "I love the colours. So vibrant. I'm surprised you didn't paint yourself in there with me."

"I wanted to capture your beauty," I said, looking at her, not the painting. I still couldn't entirely do her justice.

She smiled at me, and I sensed that she wanted me to kiss her. There was something about the way she inclined her head to the side and parted her lips. I leaned in and kissed her softly, running my fingers through her hair. She wrapped her arms around my neck. It was hard to pull away, but I eventually managed.

"I'm so glad you like it," I said. "I don't usually show people my paintings of them."

"Why not?" she asked. "Being painted is one of the highest compliments someone could pay you."

"Do you really think that?" I asked. "I'm thrilled to hear you say that. I'm delighted you like the painting."

"Thank you," she said.

"Now, every time you look at it, you'll see how I see you. And you'll remember that I think you're incredible."

She played with a strand of my hair. "You're really romantic, you know that?"

"Am I?" I asked and kissed her again. "I guess you could say that I've been preoccupied with a certain woman in my life lately..."

"Oh, and is she nice?"

"She's wonderful." I smiled. "She's been helping me through a really tough time."

"How have you been holding up? With Ghost being gone, I mean."

"I ask Gen every day for photos and videos. She's been easing up and sending me daily updates. I'm glad for that, but it's not the same as having her here with us."

"I understand." She squeezed my arm. "Keep messaging her. Eventually, she might let you visit, and then we can go from there."

"I hope so," I said. Tears pricked my eyes. "It's been far too long since I gave Ghost a hug or kiss on the nose. But at least I know she's being taken care of, and she seems comfortable."

"She's safe, and that's the most important thing. She might not be with the best human on the planet right now, but she's safe. And we'll get her back."

"Thanks for comforting me," I said.

Narisha smiled. "I'm always here for you. I hope you know that."

"Yeah. Thank you." I hugged her. "I'm glad you're here."

"I'm glad that you're part of my life now."

"And I don't intend to go anywhere," I replied.

"Even if polyamory is a little scary?"

"I can face the fear if you're by my side."

"That's a good sign for our relationship," Narisha said. "I'm ecstatic things worked out with you and Eliza, too. That's important to me. She's said nothing but good things about you. She thinks you're friendly."

"That's great," I said. "I'm glad I made a good first impression."

"Does it still make you nervous?" she asked. There was dread in her eyes. I could tell she was afraid of losing me.

"It does make me nervous, yes," I said. "I've been nervous this whole time, and we've made it work. I know right now, everything seems convoluted. But I'm sure we can figure it out." I motioned to the living room. "Want to sit down?"

She smiled. "Actually, I was hoping to lay down." She motioned to the bedroom. "Do you mind?"

"Not at all!" I exclaimed. "I'm definitely down for some time relaxing with you."

"And cuddles," she added.

"And cuddles," I repeated, smiling. "I can do that for you."

"Thank you," she said, relief clear on her face.

We moved to the bedroom. Within seconds, we were wrapped up in each other as I spooned her. She smelled wonderful, as always. This time, I thought I smelled vanilla. I pressed my lips to the back of her neck, and she sighed.

"This feels really nice," she said.

I rubbed her arms. "It does."

"I'm glad I found you, you know," she said.

"I'm glad I found you, too," I replied. "Though I suppose we didn't really find each other. Mark was the one who introduced us."

"How is Mark, anyway?" she asked. "Have you seen him lately?"

I remembered the last time I had spoken with Mark. I hadn't had much time to process my emotions since then. There had been too much going on, and I had been too preoccupied with my meeting with Eliza and Narisha to think much about what he said.

"We saw each other a few days ago, actually," I said. "Right before I drove over to meet with you."

She glanced over her shoulder at me. "What did you two talk about?"

"We had a difficult conversation."

She rolled over to face me. "Why do you say that?"

"It was about our feelings for each other."

"What did Mark say?"

"He confessed that he had feelings for me but was still apprehensive about the idea of a relationship. He says he's willing to try things out with me, though."

"Wow, I didn't expect that," Narisha said. "He's always been so uninvolved. Even emotionally."

"He told me that he actually felt disposable to you," I said. "And that it hurt his feelings."

She raised a brow. "Really? That's odd. He never expressed anything like that to me. But the reality is that he is a more casual presence in my life. I wouldn't call him disposable, though."

"I understand. I think he wants to feel like his relationships are meaningful."

"Do you think you'll continue the conversation next time you see him?"

"I don't know," I said. "I hope so."

"I know your lifestyles may seem opposite, but if you care for each other, that's what matters most."

"I know. And I want to keep seeing him. I think that I can adapt. I've done a decent job so far."

"You'll work things out." She smiled. "Besides, I think it's already clear that I like you a lot. And that I want to be with you. So at least you have that."

My breath was coming in short. "I want to be with you, too."

"Then maybe we can make this work," she said.

I thought about spending the night with her. The reality was that sleeping with her next to me was one of the most relaxing experiences I'd had in the last few years. There were very few people I could sleep next to calmly, and Narisha was one of them.

"Thank you for being so great, babe," she said. "Did you know that you blush every time I call you 'babe'?"

My hands flew up to my face. "Do I?"

"You do. It's adorable, actually."

"I really like it when you call me that," I said.

"Then I'll be sure to call you that more often."

"I'm so glad we met," I said. "I never would have considered polyamory before Mark introduced me to it and you. And even though it's been kind of rough so far, I can see the benefits. The most important one being that I get to be with you."

"Me and whoever else you want," she said.

"To be honest, I'm focused on you and Mark right now," I said.

"And there's nothing wrong with that," she replied. "I know a lot of couples get monogamish during the first couple months of dating."

"Monogamish?" I repeated.

"It's like being open but having monogamist tendencies."

"I'll have to start writing all these words down."

"It's okay if you forget," she said. "It's a lot to remember. When people are infatuated, even when they're polyamorous, they can get a little possessive. Not everyone is like this, mind you, but a few are. I know I am. When I first start dating someone, they're all I can think about. I want all their attention for myself."

"Does that mean you were jealous of Mark?" I asked.

"No, not at all," she said. "Because I knew Mark. But if there was someone else you were seeing, I'd probably be a tiny bit jealous of them."

"I'm glad to know I'm not the only one, then," I said. "I felt insecure with Eliza. I thought she'd ask you to leave me, and you'd do it."

"No way," she said quickly. "I like you way too much to stop dating you now. I want to see where this goes."

"So do I," I replied. "More than anything."

"Then we'll see where it goes," she said, taking my hand. "And I'll try not to get too intense on you."

"Intense?"

"I get a little intense with people I like."

"How?"

"I get feelings fast. And I don't shy away from that."

"So do I. And I definitely have feelings for you."

She laughed. "I'm so happy about that. Things happen differently in the polyamory world. If it's our time, it's our time. We just have to make the best of it."

"I think as long as we both want this, then it's our time," I said.

"You're right." She pulled out her phone. "I should head out now and catch Eliza once she's off work."

"Go ahead and talk to her. I know how important your time with her is, and I don't want to get in the way."

"Speaking of Eliza, she was wondering if you'd like to join us for a movie night sometime soon."

I imagined all three of us sitting together, huddled under a blanket, watching a movie. It certainly sounded cozy, but I was worried I would feel left out seeing them being coupley together. What if they held hands during the movie, and I got jealous? Would I ruin the entire night? Or would it go smoothly like our first meeting had? I decided the only way to find out was to go and see for myself.

"I'd like that," I said. "Tell her thank you for inviting me."

She kissed me. "All right. I'll call you when I'm done, okay?"

"Please do," I said.

"I'm really grateful to have you in my life," she said. "I don't have many friends to rely on. But I know you'll be there for me when I need you."

"I will be," I promised.

She got out of bed. "Thanks again, Bells. I'll see you."

"Bye!"

When I heard the door shut, I threw my head back on the pillow. It had been an exhausting day, and I felt like I needed a nap. But I also wanted to keep working on my painting. Seeing Narisha get excited over the painting only made me want to finish it more—for her—so she could hang it up on her wall and think of me each time she walked past it.

I got out of bed, gathered all my painting tools, and resumed working on the piece.

My second meeting with Eliza was a bit less stressful than my first. I wasn't worried she would hate me or that I'd be ejected from Narisha's life if I didn't "pass the test." I took a cab so I wouldn't have a nervous breakdown driving over. My irrational thoughts of jealousy were less powerful now. In their place were fears about Eliza not liking me or disagreeing with me on important topics. There was still so much for me to learn, and I felt like I was fumbling my way through the waters of polyamory without hope in sight.

Eliza had graciously invited me to meet at her place. My first impression of her house, from the outside, was that it was tall—it was a four-storey duplex. Inside, on the ground floor, was a hallway. As she welcomed us inside, I spotted at least a dozen pairs of boots and heels lined up against the wall. One pair I recognized as Narisha's, but the rest were too sparkly for her to ever wear. The collection must have belonged to Eliza.

Narisha was waiting for me inside. She was dressed in high-waisted jeans and a black, long-sleeved shirt. Her hair was pulled up into a ponytail, and I noticed her nails were painted red and neatly manicured for the evening. Eliza was dressed more casually this time, wearing jeans and a beige blouse.

"I'm so glad you could make it," Eliza said, pulling me in for a hug.

I hugged her back. I was pleasantly surprised by the affection. "Thank you for having me over."

"Yes, thank you for hosting," Narisha said. She squeezed Eliza's arm and gave her a warm smile.

I hung up my jacket before we moved to the living room. The walls were painted a light blue, with photographs of the ocean hanging there. There was also a portrait of horses galloping across the sand.

"These are beautiful photos," I said.

"Narisha took all of them," Eliza replied. "Her work was too awesome not to hang up in my home."

"Agreed," I said and felt warmth spread through me.

It was nice speaking with Eliza about Narisha like this and appreciating her talents together. I could feel jealousy in the pit of my stomach, knowing they had a connection over art that we didn't share, but I suppressed it. It was getting easier and easier to push away those feelings, especially when Eliza was so kind to me.

"Normally, I like to photograph people, but there were a few times nature was calling out to me, so I had to take out my camera," Narisha said.

"Yeah," Eliza replied. "And you did a perfect job capturing the moment."

"The one with the horses is beautifully framed," I said. "Are those wild horses?"

"They are," Narisha said. "Took me a few hours to get close enough to get the shot, but I eventually did."

"Great work," I said.

"What will I do with all of these compliments?" Narisha asked. Her cheeks were red.

"Accept them gracefully, as you always do," Eliza said.

We sat down. I sat on the smaller, cream-coloured couch while Narisha and Eliza sat on the black couch in front of me.

Eliza smiled. "How have things been in your life, Bells?"

"Things have been good," I said.

"And how's the poly lifestyle treating you?"

"Still a little intimidating," I admitted. "That much hasn't changed since our first meeting. But I was much less scared about coming here tonight. I know that this isn't an interview I need to pass."

"I'm glad to hear you've relaxed a bit about hanging out with me," Eliza said. "Believe it or not, I was worried about meeting you, too."

"What? Really?" I asked in disbelief.

"I have insecurities too, you know," Eliza said. "I wondered what would happen if you didn't like me or if we didn't get along."

"I wondered the same things!" I said. "Seems we worried ourselves for nothing."

"And, of course, I was worried, too," Narisha said. "Though I wasn't worried about you two disliking each other—I figured you would get along! I just worried that Bells would let her fear get in the way. But you totally didn't. You were brave." She smiled at me. "And I appreciate you coming here again to meet with us."

"Of course. These group meetings are important to you, so I want to make sure I'm here for it," I said. "Even if I'm still struggling to see how I fit into all of this."

"What's wrong? Why don't you see how you fit in?" Narisha asked.

"I still have feelings of jealousy," I admitted. "You both have an established relationship, and, at times, I feel like I'm kind of a third wheel, so to speak."

Narisha's face fell. "Have I done something to make you feel that way?"

"Not at all!" I exclaimed. "It's more that I see how happy you two are, and there are times when I feel a little insecure about it."

"I get it," Eliza said. "When I started dating polyamorously years ago, I was also intimidated by people who were already coupled. There's this energy, right? Between them, I mean, that you know you can't match because it hasn't been long enough. Is that right?"

I nodded. It was uncomfortable admitting my true feelings. I didn't express jealousy often. Usually, it was something I hid or bottled up. But it felt good to talk about it, and Eliza seemed to understand where I was coming from.

"What you're feeling is normal," Eliza continued. "I think we've all felt it at some point if we've dated someone already in a relationship. It can feel like you're someone they're busying themselves with on the side."

"But you know I care about you, right?" Narisha asked.

"Yeah, I know you care about me." I smiled to reassure them both, as they seemed worried. "I know you like me, Eliza, and that helps a lot. You're smart, and you clearly care a lot about Narisha. We both do. That gives us something in common."

"Do you feel you have a better sense of things now?" Eliza asked.

"I think I understand how I fit in a little better," I said. "You two have this separate, loving relationship which is fulfilling for you both. I care about Narisha, and I want her to be happy. She cares about me. And Eliza, you want everything to work out between us." I paused. "It seems to me like I fit in well here."

Narisha beamed. "You do!"

"But enough about me," I said. "Let's put the spotlight on you two now. What were you up to before I got here?"

"Before you got here, I was updating Eliza about Mark," Narisha said. "Things between him and I have been uncertain for a while."

"Yes, and I was curious to know if they were still going to see each other," Eliza said.

"And what's the verdict?" I asked.

"I think I'm a little overwhelmed with partners right now," Narisha said. "Doing group meetings like this takes a lot out of me, not to mention scheduling dates with two people at once. Three seems impossible for me and my schedule."

"That's respectable," I said. "You know yourself and are respecting your own limits. Have you talked to Mark about it yet?"

"A bit, yeah," Narisha said. "More to come later. I wanted to be conscientious of his feelings after you told me he felt replaceable. I didn't want him to feel like I didn't care at all."

"He's always been a good friend, so it makes sense to avoid burning bridges," Eliza said approvingly. "You did the right thing by talking it out."

"Thank you," Narisha said. She turned to look at me. "How are things between you two these days?"

"Good," I said. "Great at times, even. Then, at other times, less great. A little more confusing."

"Why confusing?" Eliza asked.

"Well, I have feelings for him," I said timidly. "And he's a no relationships kind of guy. And sometimes, it seems like I might scare him off with my feelings."

"Scare Mark off?" Eliza laughed. "I think we're talking about two different people."

"I worry if I'm too upfront with how I feel, we'll lose what we have," I said. "I know direct communication and transparency are important in polyamory. It probably seems obvious to just talk to him."

"That's what I was thinking, yeah," Eliza said.

"And I do intend to talk to him about it... eventually." I paused. "When the time is right. It just hasn't been right yet. And with Narisha calling it quits with him, I feel I could choose a better time."

"That's considerate of you," Narisha said. "I know if I were you, I'd just be eager to get the conversation over with. But you thought about how the timing would affect him. Good job."

I smiled. "Thank you."

"I've got some news, too," Eliza said. She took a sip of her tea. "I'm seeing someone new."

"Oh!" I exclaimed. I hadn't heard about this at all through Narisha. "What are they like?"

"I met her while I was away with work," Eliza said. "This time, though, she wasn't a co-worker."

Eliza and Narisha both laughed.

"Yeah, it would've been pretty weird if everyone you dated was someone you met from work," I admitted. "So, how did you two meet?"

"We were both at a bar after work," Eliza said. "One of the last lesbian bars in town. And we got talking. She's what I would call a 'comet partner.'"

"What's that?" I asked.

"It's someone you see now and then who flies through your life like a comet," Narisha replied. "They're not constant like other partners. For example, I know Eliza will always be around because we've made a commitment as primaries. But comets come and go."

"When they're with us, though, it's always special," Eliza added. "Like a shooting star."

I giggled. "These polyamory terms can be pretty cute sometimes."

"Yeah," Narisha said. "Either cute or science-sounding."

"It's all the Latin and Greek getting mixed together," Eliza said. "It can get confusing."

"Well, thank you for explaining the concept of a comet to me," I said. "I'm always glad to learn more."

"No problem," Eliza said. "So, what would you like to do with the rest of the evening? I was thinking we could throw on a movie."

"Do you like *But I'm a Cheerleader*?" Narisha asked. "It's a classic, and we've been meaning to rewatch it."

"How many times have you watched it together now?" I asked.

"Too many times to count," Eliza admitted.

"Not that many," Narisha said. "Maybe, like, four times. But always with other people so we can see their reactions. It's more fun that way."

"I'd like to watch it," I said.

I moved to the couch opposite where I was sitting and sat next to Narisha. We all squeezed together so we'd fit. The movie played on a mounted flatscreen TV, and it was admittedly very funny, although the themes of forced coming out and conversion therapy were stressful. I peeked at Narisha laughing a few times throughout the movie and caught her peeking back at me. We smiled at each other. Eliza seemed completely absorbed by the film despite having watched it several times.

When it was over, Narisha turned to me. "Would you like a ride home?"

"Yeah, that would be great." I got up and looked at Eliza. "Thanks so much for having me over. It was great to hang out with you two again."

"Thanks for coming to movie night!" Eliza said. "Maybe we'll do it again sometime."

"Sounds good." I hugged her. "Have a good night!"

When Narisha and I were in the car, she held my hand and gave it a squeeze. "You did great tonight."

"Thank you. I'm glad we all get along so well."

"It doesn't always happen that way, but when it does, it's wonderful," she said. "I think I saw some compersion in you tonight."

"I did feel good. And I was happy to see you happy. I'd say it counts."

Narisha laughed. "I know it's not always easy for you to hang out in groups, but I had a blast."

"So did I."

The next day, I decided to visit Mark. I was dreading the conversation we were going to have about where our relationship was going. It was plenty of stress atop keeping in touch with Gen and freaking out every time her name appeared on my phone's screen. But it needed to be done for my peace of mind. I might not have been able to get my cat back then, but I could face Mark. I took a deep breath as I hopped into my car to visit him. I'd need to be somewhat collected for this talk.

I knocked once I arrived. He opened it within seconds, smiling. The fact that he was happy to see me made it worse. I wondered if he knew what was coming. That we were about to talk about feelings and that it might get heavy.

"Hey," I said.

"Hey," he replied, opening the door. "Please come in!"

I walked into his apartment. It had become so familiar: a place where I'd be safe and where I could confide in someone. Almost like a second home. His apartment was stylish. He had leather couches, chic wall décor, and fresh flowers at the table. It struck me the first time I visited that he cared about aesthetics and appearances. My apartment was messier than his. I should've known the day I first walked in that we were two completely different people. He was organized and focused, whereas I was always more scattered, never planning ahead. I just followed my instincts wherever they led.

"What brings you over?" he asked with a worried edge to his voice.

"I wanted to talk," I replied. I pointed at his couch. "Can we sit?"

"Sure," he said, flopping onto the couch. When I sat, he moved to wrap his arm around my shoulder, but I shied away. "Is something wrong?"

My nerves were getting the best of me. I could feel my lower lip bleed from how often I had been biting it. "Actually, that's the reason I came here."

"Because I put my arm around you when we're sitting down together?" he asked teasingly. "I didn't realize that was a problem. I thought you and I were close enough now that those things wouldn't be an issue."

"I don't think we're closer now," I said. "In fact, I think we're further apart than ever."

He frowned. "Why?"

"We don't want the same things," I said. "You want a relationship that's essentially a glorified friends-with-benefits arrangement, and I want more. We're incompatible."

He sighed, looking deflated. "That's what you've come here to say, then? I thought we said we'd give this a chance since we have feelings for each other."

"Yes, but what use are feelings if you don't act on them?" I shot back. "I don't know if I can risk it. Not when I'd be waiting around forever for you to love me back. It's not who I am. You know that. We've been friends for a while now. You know I'm a hopeless romantic."

He ran a hand through his hair. "I'm feeling very emotional, and I'm not thinking straight. But, Bells, I don't think this needs to be it for us. I don't think it needs to end here." I listened for any bitterness in his voice but couldn't detect any. He just seemed disappointed. "It's been a long couple of weeks," he said with a heavy sigh.

I hugged him, and he hugged me back. It was longer than I expected. I looked him in the face. "Hey. Are we good?"

"I don't want to just be your friend," he said. "I know that's what you're going to ask me. To be your friend since I don't usually do relationships. But honestly, I can't. I can't do it." He took my hand. "What I feel for you is real. Whether you like it or not. Just because I don't want to do all that coupley stuff that you like doesn't change how real my feelings are for you. They're stronger than any feelings I've had for anyone in a while. And you're going to throw it away?"

Did he really like me that much? So much that he couldn't bear to consider friendship with me? "I didn't realize you felt so strongly about me."

He laughed nervously. It was a sound I had never heard, and it made him seem younger. "I didn't, either. Not until you started pulling away. And then I just kept thinking, 'Damn, I wish Bells was here.' I even found strands of your hair on my pillow, and it..." he paused, and I could tell he was considering his words carefully. "It... broke my heart."

"Broke your heart?" I repeated slowly. "How could that be? I thought..."

"Yeah, I know. I haven't been upfront about my feelings. Not really. I guess I hid the intensity from you because you're so consumed by this new relationship with Narisha. But honestly, Bells, the truth is... I want to be your partner. Whatever that means."

"So, you're willing to reconsider everything you said you weren't into?"

"Yes." He ran a hand through his hair. "I still want to be alone. Live alone. Be independent. Have my own life. But I want you in it. With me."

"But how?" I asked, feeling my face burn. "How could we make it work?"

"I'm not the first one to feel this way," he said. "It's called solo poly. I want to be with you. I just don't want to be your live-in partner."

He kissed me, and I kissed him back. My emotions were roiling inside of me. I hadn't expected us to kiss today. And yet, here we were on his couch in each other's arms.

He rested his forehead against mine. "I don't want to lose you," he whispered.

I closed my eyes tightly. "You won't."

"Are you sure?" My eyes weren't open, but I could tell he was watching me intently.

"Yes." I looked at him then. His eyes were wide and fearful, but there was a hint of hope in his parted lips.

"So, you'll keep seeing me?"

"Yes."

His eyes were wide and innocent. "Even though I may not give you everything you want?"

I didn't know how to respond, so I said, "We have each other. That's enough."

He kissed me softly. "That's all I needed to hear. Thank you."

I felt elated, confused, scared, and panicked all at once. I pulled away from him. "I'm happy we could talk this out."

He still held onto my hand. "Same."

I had never seen him so vulnerable before. There had always been a barrier between us, a wall of coy flirtation. But this truly was Mark. This was the person I had searched for this whole time. The person who could feel and openly admit what he wanted. The person who was afraid to let me go.

"I need to get going," I said. "I'm going to the park to see Narisha. But I'll see you again soon."

He cleared his throat, and his voice came out thick. "Sounds good."

"I'll text you, okay?" I said. "I promise. We'll talk more later."

He smiled. "Okay."

It was a beautiful day for a walk in the park. The sun shone brightly, and a few lazy clouds floated across the sky. The grass seemed greener and more vibrant than usual, the air was fresh, and a few dog walkers were strolling down the path. I sat on one of the wooden benches and waited for Narisha to appear.

I had no idea what to expect from her this afternoon. I wish she had texted me more or at least called, but she had been busy with Eliza. I couldn't begrudge her that. I hadn't had the chance to fill her in completely about Mark, but I had sent her a few messages explaining what had been said before I left to meet her.

I noticed her walking toward me from across the park. She was barefoot, holding her sandals in one hand. She had a wide smile on her face. She wore a black maxi dress with a purse hung over her shoulder, and her sunhat completed the look, making her look elegant. I was wearing a dress, too, but nothing compared to hers. Mine was a simple black dress that ended at my knees. I regretted not wearing something sleeveless.

"Hello, beautiful," she said as she sat down next to me and then kissed me.

"You taste like strawberries," I said.

She motioned to her purse. "I bought a few fresh ones at the market. Would you like one?"

"Would I ever!" I exclaimed. She took a strawberry out of her purse and handed it to me. I bit into it enthusiastically. It was incredibly sweet. For a moment, I forgot my worries. "It's perfect."

"It's good to know tasty fruit can cheer you up so easily," she noted with a smile as she donned her sandals.

"You cheer me up easily," I shot back. "The fruit is an added bonus."

"Do I really?"

"Yes," I said. "Especially when you greet me with a kiss. That's my favourite part."

"My kisses?"

"Yes. I love your kisses."

I think I saw her blush. "I love yours, too."

"Then we will have to keep kissing, won't we?"

"That would be ideal," she said.

"What a beautiful day to spend time with a gorgeous woman."

"Would you like to walk?" I asked.

"Sure," she said.

We both stood and walked arm in arm. It had been a while since I had shown public displays of affection with a woman. It was always nerve-racking because I was hyper-aware of how people looked at us. I knew it was unlikely anybody would harass us, but it was always in the back of my mind. Instead of focusing on other people, I tried to focus on the warm feeling of her arm resting in mine. That comforted me.

"So," Narisha started. "Tell me about your conversation with Mark."

"I thought we were incompatible. But we aren't okay just being friends. We both want more."

"It's good that you figured that out," she said. "But how did the rest go?"

"In the end, we decided to keep seeing each other. I'm ecstatic that things are resolved now. That's one more thing I don't have to worry about."

"I see. It's good that you cleared things up a bit." She looked away from me. "I couldn't see him again with everything going on. I needed to focus my attention on what was most important."

"I know you mentioned this at Eliza's place, but did it have anything to do with me?" I asked.

"No," she said weakly, glancing back at me. "Well, not exactly. I mean, you're part of the reason, but you're not the entire reason. I really like you, and I want things to work. I don't have time for casual relationships right now."

"Do you think we're in a relationship?" I asked, feeling like my insides were going to melt. Normally, I wouldn't be so brave, but she had called what we had a "relationship" several times now.

She held my hand. "I think we can be girlfriends if that's what you want."

"I do want that," I said. "There's nothing I want more."

"You're so cute," she whispered and kissed me.

This time was different. Earlier, her kiss had been quick. This kiss was deep and passionate. Her fingers lightly ran through my hair. By the time she was done, I was entirely breathless.

"I'm so happy," I said and hugged her.

Her hat began sliding off before she fixed it. "Me, too."

I touched her face tenderly. I didn't care about the passersby who were staring at us. I only cared about her beautiful brown eyes.

We continued walking. The breeze tousled Narisha's curls gently.

"So much has happened in so little time," she said. "Things are changing with Mark, and now you and I are official."

I winced. "I hope we're not moving too fast for you."

"No, not at all!" she said. "I understand why you'd be worried about that, but we're fine. We've been seeing each other for a while now."

"I usually move much quicker," I said. "But my last breakup made me want to go a little slower, I guess."

"I've moved on quickly before, too," she replied.

"I know not everyone takes as long as I do to heal," I admitted. "That's probably one of my biggest flaws."

"I think it's one of your biggest strengths," Narisha replied. "The fact that you feel things so strongly is beautiful. You translate that to your art. You create truly spectacular pieces."

"I'm glad you think so," I said. "I normally don't show my paintings to people. Not the ones about love."

"Why not?"

"Well, to be honest, by the time I finish the paintings, they've usually broken up with me."

"Oh." Narisha looked sorry for me. "That sucks."

"It does," I said. "But I think creating art is part of my healing process."

"Well, I'm not going anywhere," she said. "You won't have to worry about that."

I squeezed her hand. "You don't know how glad I am to hear you say that."

"You're afraid of people leaving you, aren't you?" she asked.

We turned a corner as a cyclist passed by. I took a moment to compose myself. Those kinds of questions scared me. "A little."

"I noticed," she said. "You act as if everyone in your life is temporary. So, you save them in a painting."

"I try to replicate precious moments in my paintings," I said. "Fleeting moments. And yes, moments I'm afraid to lose."

"So, you were afraid to lose that moment we shared at the gala," she said. "That's why you painted it."

"Basically, yeah," I said, embarrassed I was so transparent. "I thought you looked so beautiful that night at the gala, and you were so into me that I wanted to capture that moment forever."

"It's even better than a camera, I think," she said. "Because I get to see myself through your eyes. And I like what I see."

"So do I," I said, playing with a strand of her hair. "A lot."

"I hope you don't mind me asking this, but did you paint one of Gen?"

"I did," I said. "I painted a portrait of us sitting on the couch together at her house, laughing. It was the first time we said 'I love you' to each other."

"Wow. That's deep. You told me painting was a way for you to hold on to lost memories. I think we all do that in some way. Yours is just more poetic."

"I was thinking of throwing the canvas out, actually," I said. "I don't really want to keep anything that reminds me of her."

"You shouldn't throw it out," Narisha said quickly. "It's your art. It may cause you pain now, but later in life, you might look at it in a different light."

"How?" I asked incredulously. "Gen isn't exactly close to me anymore."

"You might look at that relationship as part of the journey," she said. "Just like I'm part of your journey."

"Most paintings I've made of people I've loved have been sweet. Believe it or not, not all my breakups ended as badly as it did with Gen. I'm still friends with most of my exes, actually. That's why I don't mind keeping them. But hers..."

"Hers might not have nice feelings attached to it, but it's still something that helps you heal. You put so much effort into it. It would be a shame to throw it away."

"I don't like knowing it's there," I said.

"Then maybe the next step is to burn it," she said with a nod. "If it causes you that much distress, then maybe you're right. Maybe it's better gone." She smiled. "You've made something nicer now, anyway."

"That's true. I'm glad she and I broke up. If we hadn't, I would never have been open-minded enough to try and date you."

"That's true, isn't it?" she smiled. "Just means we should be thankful to whatever led us here."

After our walk in the park, I went home for some well-deserved rest. I needed to find some way to relax and release the emotions caught in my body. I needed to express myself with canvas and paint. I had escaped the depressing cycle I was caught in, only painting lost loves. I had painted Narisha, a new and beautiful person in my life, and she loved it. It was a time for new beginnings. And it was time to put the past to rest. I would have time to spend with my friends once I was done.

Before I got to work, I texted Alex.

> Me: Hey. Would you and Nina mind coming over for a bit?

Her reply was instantaneous.

> Alex: Of course. Whatever you need. We'll be there.

> Me: Great. I'll text you when I'm free.

I retrieved the painting of Gen I had shoved into the corner. Bitterness burst from my heart and spread through my chest. It hurt just to look at her. I thought of everything she had done to me and all the ways she had betrayed and disrespected me. There was no reason to hold on any longer. Our relationship was over. There was no possibility of friendship. And so, as much as I may have enjoyed reliving the memories of our love, those memories were no longer useful.

I walked over to the fireplace. One of the reasons I had chosen this apartment was because the fireplace seemed so warm and cozy. Now, it would serve another purpose entirely: to destroy what I had created. I filled the fireplace with firewood, set it ablaze, and gripped the canvas tight. I hesitated for a moment. Was this the right move? Did I have to destroy the painting? I had put so much effort into it. And if every artist destroyed the paintings they no longer loved, we'd lose countless great works of art. But I shook my head. No, I couldn't keep it. It was just too painful. I would replace it with my new, happy memories. I opened the windows to let in the fresh air.

I threw the canvas into the fire and watched it burn. I don't know how long I sat there. I couldn't tear my eyes away from the blue colours erupting into red and the ash curling up at the base. As our faces were erased by the flames, I tried to let go. Let go of all the feelings of love, tenderness, and yearning I felt for Gen. Those feelings weren't useful anymore. They just got in the way of what was important—moving on to better things.

Once satisfied the painting was gone, I left my place on the floor and pulled out a fresh, blank canvas. I wanted to express how I felt. I didn't want it to only reflect my positive emotions. I wanted it to be all-encompassing. I needed to come up with an image that could represent how I felt about Narisha, how I felt about Mark, the growing pains of polyamory, and my elation at falling in love once again, but with more than one person.

I wanted Narisha and Mark featured in the painting. They were two beautiful subjects that I could not leave out of the piece. I wasn't certain if I wanted to include myself, though. I started by sketching both of them and let the muse take me wherever she willed.

I pulled two photos of them from my camera roll and flipped back and forth as my pencil flowed across the blank sheet. First, I drew Narisha's oval face with her full lips, wide eyes, and curly hair. Then, I drew Mark with his half-smile, tousled hair, and deep trustworthy eyes. There they were: the two people I cared about most right then. The two people I could envision my future with.

Narisha had become my rock in such a short time, keeping me steady and on my feet when times were tough. She had shown that she was reliable and that I could call or text her at any time, and she would be there for me. I couldn't ask for more. She had committed to me. That meant a lot.

I sketched my face between Narisha and Mark. I was what brought them together now. I drew the rest of our bodies, with Narisha and Mark both facing me and my gaze set on the viewer. I drew Narisha in a dress and Mark in his familiar black jeans and dress shirt. I was dressed in the outfit I had worn to the art gala. I drew a thread that wrapped around our forearms and connected us.

I brought out my paints. I wanted the background to be a deep blue to represent both the sadness I was experiencing and the healing journey I had embarked on. The sun was above us, shining brightly. I used gold for that, and it leaked down to the thread that bound us. Our connection was radiant in the chaos of movement surrounding us. Our connection would steer us forward. It would keep us together and keep us strong. I added shadows behind us, representing the challenges that our polyamorous lifestyle could bring. But the light was ever-present. As long as we stayed strong, we would keep those ghosts at bay.

After four hours, I was satisfied with my work. I texted Alex when I was nearly done and asked her to come over. I set the easel next to the window so the morning light could catch the colours. It always helped to look at a piece with a fresh perspective instead of working all through the night to finish it.

I sprung from the couch when I heard a knock on the door. I rushed to open it. Alex and Nina stood in the hallway, dressed in their usual clashing outfits. Alex's hair was down and curled, which was surprising. She was still wearing yoga pants, but these ones seemed fancier. Nina had done her hair, as well. It was curled, and I noticed she had cut her bangs. I realized with dawning horror that I had most likely interrupted a date.

"Wow, I feel... underdressed," I said.

"Don't worry about it," Alex said, pushing past me and striding into the apartment.

"But you look like you two were on a date!" I said, following her to the couch.

Nina shut the door behind us. "We were, but you're more important than that."

I groaned and shoved my face into my hands. "I'm sorry for ruining your date, guys."

"You didn't ruin anything," Alex said gently. "We came here of our own free will, didn't we?"

"Yes, but..." I started.

"But nothing," Alex interrupted. "We'd rather be here with you, knowing you're okay, than at home worrying."

I smiled shakily. "Thank you. I appreciate it."

Nina looked pointedly at my fingers. "Have you been painting?"

I looked down at my hands. I had forgotten to wash them. I jumped up and ran to the kitchen sink. "Sorry. Forgot to clean up."

"It's okay," she replied. "What were you working on?"

I motioned with my head to the easel as I scrubbed the paint off my hands. "A new piece."

"Another painting for a lost love?" Alex asked.

"Nope," I said. I walked back to the couch and sat between the couple. "This one is for new loves. And hope."

"Huh. That's different from your usual," Alex observed.

"I think it's time for a change, honestly," I said.

Alex placed a hand on my shoulder. "You mentioned in your text that things had been rough today. Do you want to talk about it?"

Nina took my hand and squeezed it.

"It's okay," Nina said softly. "You're safe here with us."

"I know." I was getting choked up. "Everything has just been... a lot this week."

"I imagine things moving forward with Narisha has kept your mind occupied."

"There's that. And things with Mark have been consuming me, too."

Nina got up and inspected my newest painting. "Is that why he's in this one?"

I nodded. "We had a talk. An emotional one."

"How did it go?" Alex asked.

I smiled. "He said he has feelings for me."

"What changed?" Alex asked.

"He said he wants some sort of relationship with me. Just not a conventional one."

"Well, you've certainly thrown conventionality to the wind recently," Alex noted.

"So, you're not going to warn me to be careful?"

"We've done enough of that, don't you think?" Alex asked.

"True. I still don't entirely understand what Mark expects we'd be. He says he wants to be a solo polyamorist. Someone who lives alone, doesn't necessarily have a primary, and just..."

"Dates a bunch of people?" Nina added.

"Yeah," I said. "Basically."

"And does any of this bother you?" Alex asked. "It's not like your family would be overjoyed to meet all your partners, anyway. Does he have to live with you to make it official?"

I frowned. "I don't know. Things were different with my past relationships. We'd do all the normal things. Meet each other's friends. Mark doesn't want to do any of that. But he cares about the things that matter."

"Like what?" Nina asked.

"Like love, companionship, and commitment," I replied.

"Does your relationship have to be publicly acknowledged for you to enjoy it?" Nina asked.

Nina seemed to understand the workings of polyamory better than I did. "I suppose I don't need it to be publicly acknowledged to enjoy my relationship with him."

"So there," Alex said. "Maybe dating someone who is solo poly isn't bad after all."

"Besides," Nina added. "You also have Narisha. And you two seem to be getting intimate."

"We are," I said. "In fact, on our walk today, she said we could call ourselves girlfriends."

"Really?" Alex shrieked. She hugged me, pushing me into Nina's lap as we all laughed.

"That's wonderful!" Nina said.

I felt so warm and comfortable in their embrace that I never wanted to let go. I was so thankful I had such great friends to support me.

"I know this wasn't what you two probably envisioned for me," I said, resting my head on Nina's lap.

Alex smiled. I was surprised by how warm her eyes were. "I just want you to be happy. That's what matters most to me. If you're happy with Narisha and Mark, then I won't fault you." A familiar glare settled on her face. "But if either of them hurt you..."

"We know, we know." Nina raised a finger to silence her girlfriend. "You'll kick their butts or something to that effect. Now isn't the time to make threats, my love. We should be celebrating her new relationships!"

"Yes! We should do something," Alex said. "This is the beginning of a new journey for you."

"I think I know how I need to celebrate," I whispered. They both looked at me expectantly. I smiled shyly. "I need you guys to hold me. Do you think you can do that? I've been such a mess since Gen took Ghost from me, and I haven't had time to relax and enjoy the moment. I'd like to do that with you two."

"Nothing wrong with a good old cuddle puddle," Nina said as she wrapped her arms around my shoulders. Alex settled next to me, and I closed my eyes.

This is what I needed: to be surrounded by the warm, comforting presence of my friends. Tonight, I would rest easy knowing I had people around me who loved me and wanted what was best for me.

ELEVEN

When I woke up the next morning, I felt rested and refreshed. Despite my anxiety about Ghost, I was able to have fun with my friends the night before. They had offered the comfort I had direly needed. When I arose from bed, I was determined to get my cat back. This had gone on for far too long, and I was entitled to visit her to see how she was doing. I decided I was going to go to Gen's place and confront her.

Thankfully, I didn't have to do it alone. Narisha offered to come with me as soon as I texted her my plans.

"I'll be here for you, whatever comes our way," she said.

We drove downtown. Gen lived in an apartment far fancier than mine in the city centre. She even had a concierge. She had started a new job as an architect. Obviously, it paid better than being a painter. I had gotten her address because I had to deliver some of her things after we broke up. I was glad I already had it because asking now would be awkward.

Narisha and I stood in the foyer. She held my hand. I was scared, but I felt stronger with her by my side.

"Are you sure you're ready to do this?" she asked.

"Yes," I said. "I'm just terrified of confrontation."

"I'll be right there with you," she said and squeezed my hand.

"I'm not even sure Gen will let us in," I said shakily.

"We have to try," Narisha said. "That's all we can do."

I took a deep breath and called up to Gen's apartment. I was so nervous that the ringing over the speakers sounded deafening. Eventually, she picked up.

"Hello?" Gen said.

"It's Isabelle," I said. "I'm here to get Ghost back."

Gen laughed. "Seriously? You're delusional if you think I'm letting you up here."

"She doesn't belong with you," I said. "You know that. Just give her back. You've caused me enough pain."

"No way," she said. "Now leave my building."

"We're not leaving without Ghost," Narisha said. "So let us in."

"Ooh, you brought your little girlfriend," Gen crooned. "That won't help you."

"How is Ghost?" I asked. "Are you even taking care of her?"

"She's being annoying right now, actually," Gen grumbled. "She pissed all over my bed this morning."

"She probably wants to come home," I said.

"Ugh, now *you're* the annoying one," Gen said. "If I let you take her, will you promise to stop texting me?"

"I was only texting you because you stole my cat!" I exclaimed.

"Fine, fine, whatever," she muttered. "Come on up."

The door opened. The concierge, who likely overheard our entire conversation, looked flustered. I smiled at him apologetically. I didn't mean to cause drama in the lobby.

"I'm proud of you," Narisha said. "I know how hard that must have been."

"The hardest part is coming up," I said as we walked toward the stairs. "I can deal with her over the phone, but she's terrifying in person."

"Was she always like that?" Narisha asked as we headed upstairs.

"No," I said. "I never realized she had a temper until our breakup. She hid it from me our entire relationship."

"Sometimes you think you know someone, but you really don't," Narisha said.

"Even after being close with them," I said. "Yeah. It sucks."

We reached the second floor and headed to Gen's apartment. I knocked on the door. A few moments later, Gen walked out of her apartment, scowling. I could hear Ghost meowing from inside.

"Is she okay?" I asked, trying to see past the door.

"She's fine," Gen muttered. "She had fun pissing all over the apartment this morning."

I met her gaze. "So, I take it you don't want her anymore?"

"She's more trouble than she's worth," Gen sniffed. "She scratched the hell out of me yesterday and this morning, in addition to pissing all over the place."

I noticed the scratch marks on her arm for the first time. They looked red and angry. Ghost must have been displeased if she left those.

"You didn't have to bring a bodyguard, you know," Gen said, looking at Narisha.

"She's not my bodyguard," I said. "She's my girlfriend. And she's here to support me."

"Support you?" Gen laughed. "Why would you need support? Is coming here so overwhelming for you?"

"You know exactly why this is overwhelming for me," I said. Anger gripped me. "How can you act like you don't know me? We dated for a year, Gen! You knew me better than anyone on the planet. And now you're acting like you don't know me at all. But you know exactly how much this is stressing me out. You know how much I love Ghost."

I pressed my nails into my palm to keep myself from losing it. She was being incredibly disrespectful. It was hard to imagine that, only a few months ago, I had considered Gen to be my closest friend in the world. Now she was the last person I ever wanted to see.

"I thought I knew you, too," Gen shot back. "Then you started dating this girl, and now I don't know what to think. You've changed."

"I didn't change her," Narisha said. "I just accepted her for who she is."

"That's such bullshit," Gen spat. "You don't even know her. How long have you even been dating? Get over yourself. You're just the newest, shiniest thing in her life. You'll be dull soon enough."

"Hey!" I exclaimed. "You don't get to talk to her like that."

"And why not?" Gen asked, her eyes wide with fury. "You turned your back on me to go date her. Why shouldn't I hate her?"

I frowned. I didn't like how much noise we were making. One of her neighbours would likely make a complaint. I mustered the courage to continue. "Because that's immature! Do you hear yourself? Do you seriously believe what you're saying right now?"

"All I know is that I gave you the option to explore the polyamorous lifestyle with me, and you said no." She glared at Narisha. "For her."

"Yes, I did," I said. "End of story."

"Don't you have a girlfriend, Gen?" Narisha asked. "Maybe it's time you focus your energy on *her* instead of your ex."

"Shut up," Gen snapped. "You don't get to tell me how to live my life."

I had waited long enough. I could see Ghost trying to slip past Gen's legs. I couldn't just stand by while my baby suffered. I dove to my knees, and Ghost came running to me. I picked her up and cradled her to my chest.

"See? She wants to be with me."

"Give her back!" Gen yelled, lunging.

Narisha stepped in the way. "I don't think so."

Gen glared at her, and there was a heavy silence as we stood in the hallway. I could feel Ghost's heartbeat racing against my hand as I held her to me.

"You should back off, Gen," Narisha said. "We've got Ghost. That's why we came here. We'll leave you alone if you let us have her."

"You seriously couldn't come here and do it yourself?" she asked me, ignoring Narisha entirely. "How pathetic."

"Ghost isn't happy with you. You must see that. She wouldn't be scratching you like this if she didn't want to come home."

"Fine, take her back then." Gen glared at me. "You've got your stupid cat back. You're welcome."

"Can this be it, please?" I asked, feeling exhausted. I was relieved to finally have my cat back, but I was wary. Gen was still acting irrationally, and I didn't want her showing up at my place unannounced again.

"What do you mean, 'can this be it'?" Gen asked.

"Can we stop fighting, or whatever this is?" I asked. "It's really tiring, and to be honest, I doubt either of us has enough time or energy to keep it going. So why don't we shake hands and leave it at that?"

"You think it's that easy?" Gen asked incredulously. "You think I'll just forgive you after everything?"

"What are you talking about?" I asked.

Gen rolled her eyes. "I'm talking about the absolute *nerve* it took for her to reject me and date you instead."

"So, you're not willing to part on friendly terms, then," I said.

"No," Gen replied. "I guess I'm not."

Narisha stepped forward. Gen stumbled back.

"You don't know what you're missing," Narisha said. "Isabelle is a wonderful person. If she offered me friendship, I'd take it."

"Yeah, well, you're not me," Gen said boldly, though there was a hint of fear in her eyes.

"You're right," Narisha replied. "I definitely am *not* you."

"We'll be going now," I said, cradling Ghost to my chest. "Have a nice day."

"Whatever," Gen muttered. She slammed the door shut on the way back into her apartment.

"We did it!" I shrieked once she was gone. She could probably still hear me through her door, but I didn't care. I had my cat back. We confronted Gen, and I survived. And Narisha had been there for me the entire time.

"We did!" Narisha exclaimed. "Good job. You didn't back down."

"And neither did you," I noted. "Thank you for standing up for me."

She kissed my cheek. "Anytime. Want to go home?"

"Absolutely."

When we arrived at my place, Ghost had the zoomies from being away from home for so long and tore around the apartment. Narisha and I laughed at her exuberant mood.

"She's clearly happy to be home," Narisha said. "And I bet her mum is happy she's home, too."

"You have no idea," I said. "This is a huge relief."

Narisha pulled out a small black bag from her purse. "I've got something for you. To help you relax. I thought you might need it after the confrontation today."

"Do I get to open it right away?" I asked. She nodded. I took the bag from her hands and opened it. Inside was a sweet-smelling bar. It was pink and white with rose petals on its side. "You got me soap? Is this a hint or something that I should bathe more often?"

She laughed loudly. "It's not soap, silly! It's a massage bar. For us to use together."

I shot a nervous glance over to my bathroom door. "I'm not certain I have the space to do that anywhere in here."

"We can try and sit by the tub." She wrapped her arms around my waist. "Come on. Think of it as an adventure." She lifted the bar up to my eyes. "What do you say?"

"I say you're very romantic for thinking ahead and buying me a gift," I said before I kissed her.

"I know things have been a little stressful for you lately," she said. "But it all worked out, and now we're here together. And we can enjoy each other."

I took her hand in mine. "Let's try it out."

"Yay!" she exclaimed. "I'm so excited. The lady at the shop said this one was great. She said it smelled amazing and made your skin feel incredibly soft."

We made our way over to the bathroom. I sat on the edge of the tub and turned the tap. As water rushed out, Narisha turned off the lights. Only the faint glow coming from the window illuminated the room. She ran the massage bar under the water and lathered it up.

I dipped my arm in the warm water. Narisha followed suit. I rubbed the bar against my skin. It was smooth and left a pink trail up my arm. I let my fingertips play with the tiny rose petals on its surface. Narisha was right: it smelled amazing. And it felt amazing, too. Somehow, the aroma relaxed me even more than the warmth of the water.

Narisha's hands went to my shoulders. She massaged them gently, then a bit harder, digging into the knots. I melted under her touch.

"Thank you so much for this," I whispered.

"You're welcome," she said. She kissed my neck gently. "Let's take the time to enjoy each other. Properly."

I changed into a pair of fresh clothes. Narisha and I curled up on the couch together, perfectly content. My head was resting on her shoulder, and she had her arm wrapped around me.

"I'm so lucky to have you," I said.

"That makes two of us, then," Narisha replied. "Because I'm ecstatic to have you. In more ways than one."

I giggled. "Yeah. That was wonderfully relaxing."

"We should do it again sometime," she suggested.

"I'd do that every day if I could," I said.

We spent the morning cuddling in post-bath bliss.

"I love cuddling with you," she said, then laughed.

"Why are you laughing?" I asked with an amused smile.

"I'm just so happy you're with me," she said.

"I'm happy, too," I said softly.

She stared longingly at my body. I couldn't help but do the same. "I could sit here all day just telling you how pretty you are. And how soft your skin is. And how great you smell."

Ghost interrupted our romantic conversation by running into the room and knocking over a bottle of acrylic paint that I had left on the floor. I was usually more conscious of where I left my paints, but while Ghost had been away, I had been less careful. Black paint was spilling over the floor, and Ghost's white coat was splotched.

"Oh no!" I exclaimed. I leapt up from the couch and ran over to Ghost. "What a mess!"

"Can we wash it off?" Narisha asked.

"We should be able to. Damn it! I shouldn't have left the paint there."

"It's okay, we can sort this out together," Narisha said.

I grabbed some paper towels and wiped most of the paint on the floor. There were specks left, but I'd deal with those after. I picked Ghost up, and we hurried to the bathroom. The bath was still full of pink water with rose petals floating on the surface. Narisha ran the tap again so that we'd have some fresh water while I retrieved my pet-friendly shampoo. Ghost mewed softly in my arms. I knew she had been through so much and probably just wanted a good cuddle. Instead, she was being forced to do one of her least favourite activities. Ghost had never been a fan of baths.

"Shhh, it's okay," Narisha said to Ghost. She patted her on the head. Her voice was soothing, even to me. "You're going to be all right. We're just going to clean you up a bit."

I splashed some water over Ghost's fur, then lathered her in shampoo. She resisted fiercely at first, but after a pep talk from Narisha, she seemed to calm down. I smiled. Even though they didn't understand each other, Ghost knew that Narisha was someone she could trust. She was safe around both of us. She was home.

The black paint washed off. I watched as the dirty bath water drained. Ghost was back to her former state, her coat gleaming. I got the hair dryer, set it to cool, and ensured she was back to her dry and fluffy state before letting her loose in the apartment again.

While Narisha and I cleaned the remainder of the paint spill, she motioned to my tools. "So, when can I see this new painting you made?"

I looked away nervously. "I didn't think you noticed it."

"I did as soon as we walked in. You put it by the window. It's hard to miss."

"I was hoping to show it to you and Mark at the same time."

She inclined her head to the side. "Oh?"

"It's a painting for both of you. About both of you. About us, really. About my feelings and polyamory."

"Wow," she said. "Now I *really* want to see it."

She pulled out her phone and started texting.

"What are you doing?" I asked, leaning over her shoulder.

"Waking up Mark and telling him to get his butt over here." She flashed me a brilliant smile. "I don't want to be kept waiting for your next beautiful piece."

"Don't get too excited. It might not live up to expectations."

"If you made it, it's special."

I smiled and kissed her. "Thank you."

Narisha's phone dinged. She looked at it. "It's him. He says he'll leave right away. Good thing dude's an early riser, or we would've had to drag him out of bed."

"True." I crossed my arms in front of my chest. "Though honestly, I'm a little nervous about showing him the painting."

"Why?"

"The last time we spoke, things were intense."

"Because you don't know how you feel about solo polyamory?" she asked.

I nodded. "Yeah."

"I'm sure whatever connection you have with Mark can be worked out," she said. "I know he's looking for something you've never encountered before, but so was I. You adjusted. I think what really matters is how you feel about him. Do you think it's worth the challenge to be with him? Worth the emotional conversations? The processing? The jealousy?"

"I'm not an extremely jealous person," I said. "I mean, sure, I was jealous a few times. I was worried and insecure. But I generally don't mind the idea of my partners finding happiness elsewhere. I might not have experienced compersion with Mark yet, but... if it's done respectfully, I don't see why I wouldn't."

"Compersion will come with time and experience," Narisha said. "Once you see Mark talking about someone and his face lights up, you'll probably feel glad for him."

I held her close. "All I have to say is I look forward to experiencing it with you. With you by my side, I feel I can deal with whatever comes our way."

She squeezed me tightly. "And I'll be here to support you."

I tidied the apartment a little before Mark arrived. I adjusted the sheet lying over the canvas. I caught Narisha trying to peek a few times. Ghost watched us from her usual perch atop the couch.

As excited as I was to show them what I created, I was also nervous. Like I told Narisha, this would be the first time Mark and I spoke since our emotional conversation. I was glad, in a way, that time had passed. It gave us the opportunity to address this with a clear head. Hopefully, he had taken the time to think things over for himself, as well. Narisha answered the door. Mark was dressed in ripped jeans and a band T-shirt. He was holding a bouquet of roses.

"For the ladies of the house." He bowed theatrically.

I laughed and took the flowers. "Thank you, Mark. They're beautiful."

"Come on in," Narisha said. "We were just tidying up."

I put the roses in a vase filled with water and placed them on the kitchen counter. "There. They look lovely."

"I figured, given how I was summoned, I would have to bring a peace offering," he explained.

"We're not upset with you, Mark," Narisha said. "We just figured it would be good to have a conversation together. All three of us."

Mark threw himself onto the couch. "I assume things are serious between you two now?"

"Yeah," I said and reached for Narisha's hand. She smiled and interlaced her fingers with mine. I melted under the gaze of those brown eyes. "We decided we're official partners."

"Wow," he said. "That's awesome! I'm glad you found each other."

"We should thank you," I said. "Since you're the one who introduced us, after all."

"You're welcome. Now, are we going to have this discussion or what?"

Narisha laughed. "No beating around the bush with you."

"I'm just feeling restless," he explained and laughed nervously. "I'm sorry. I feel a lot of pressure coming here today."

"I wanted us all to talk about our relationships," I explained.

"Oh." He stopped fidgeting. "That's not so bad."

"I'll get us some tea, then we can get settled and start talking," I said.

Thankfully, Narisha had already thought to boil the water. I steeped the tea, and within minutes, we were all huddled up on the couch with our individual drinks. We all sipped our teas in silence for a moment, gathering our thoughts.

"So…" Mark started. "I imagine the painting over there with the sheet on it has something to do with our conversation today."

"Yeah. It's… a new piece."

"Not a lost love?" Mark asked.

Narisha wrapped an arm around my shoulders. "Nope. She's done with those for now." She winked. "She even painted me."

"Oh, I have to see that one," he said, looking at me like a pleading puppy. "May I?"

I laughed. I liked how Mark could turn any heavy conversation light. "Sure."

I went to the bedroom, fetched the painting, and showed it to him. He whistled.

"You definitely captured her spirit," he said. "It's a great painting. Good work."

"Thank you," I said, puffing with pride. "But I think I should probably show you the painting I made of both of you."

They both watched me expectantly. The moment of truth. I took a deep breath, walked to the easel, and pulled off the sheet. They both shot from the couch and stood next to me. Mark placed a hand on his chin, inspecting the painting with narrowed eyes. I couldn't interpret his facial expression. Narisha, on the other hand, was smiling. That was a good sign, at least. Showing off my work was always the hardest part, especially when it was something so intimate.

"What does the golden ribbon represent?" Mark asked.

"It's our connection," I said. "We're all bound together. Even though you and Narisha aren't dating, you're connected through friendship. And through me."

"It's beautiful," Narisha said. "I love the symbolism. A thread that connects all three of us. Our love for you."

I held my breath for a moment. Did she just say love? Neither she nor Mark had said they loved me yet. But she didn't correct herself.

I cleared my throat. "Mark? What do you think?"

"You certainly captured all of us very accurately," he said. "You're really talented at realism, Bells."

"Thank you. I wanted to draw a tumultuous background to represent the struggles of being poly. Not just jealousy and stuff, but also society's view of our lifestyle. Of my inner emotions. Of my struggles."

"And that's why the foreground is so bright?" Mark asked.

I smiled. So, he *was* engaged with the work. "Yes."

"I like it," he said finally, dropping his hand from his face.

"Why?" I asked, desperate for more than a simple compliment.

He looked me in the eyes. "Because it means you want me in your life."

I smiled. "I *do* want you in my life."

"I think this is where we talk," he said, sitting back down on the couch.

Narisha and I followed him. I sat between them both again.

"So, you want me in your life," he continued. "What does that look like?"

Narisha watched us attentively, not saying a word.

"I don't need you to be my boyfriend in the strict sense of the word," I said. "I mean, I'd still like to call you my boyfriend because it's a term of endearment for me. But I don't expect you to move in one day. I don't expect you to come to functions with me or meet my family. Narisha can do that." I glanced at her. "If she wants, that is."

"Oh, I'd like that," Narisha said.

I smiled shakily at Mark. "So, you see? Since Narisha is my partner, too, I don't need you to do all those things. She'll do them with me."

"I seem to remember you thinking that each relationship should stand on its own," Mark said. "That they shouldn't lean on each other."

"I think we'll have to lean on each other plenty moving forward," I said. "That's why I painted all three of us together. We may have separate relationships, but we're all connected. I think it'll take work as a team. And I want you to be in it. In whatever capacity you can be."

Mark took my hand. "And you're sure that will be enough for you?"

I took a risk and decided to be bold. I kissed him quickly and tenderly. "You're enough for me. I want to make this work."

I glanced back at Narisha to get her reaction. She smiled in approval. Compersion instead of jealousy.

Mark's eyes had gone distant for a moment. It was written plainly on his face. He really had feared losing me.

I squeezed his hand. "You won't lose me, Mark. I'm here to stay."

He kissed me. "Hope so."

Narisha laughed. "I think we need to dial down the kissing."

"I second that," I said.

Narisha grabbed me by the back of my shirt and pulled me back. "It's talking time."

I laughed. "All right, all right."

I was happy. Here I was, sitting next to two people who cared for me deeply. They cared enough to put up with my emotions, my unfamiliarity with polyamory, my mental illness, and every other thing that society had labelled as undesirable.

"How do we make this work?" I asked.

"I think a schedule would be helpful," Narisha said. "I'm busy most weekdays with class but free on the weekends."

"My schedule is pretty wide open," Mark said. "So, I can work around Narisha's schedule."

"You could come over while I paint, and we could work together," I suggested. "And spend the nights together."

Mark smiled. "That sounds like a good compromise. And maybe I could get one weekday a month. Just to switch things up." He turned to Narisha. "Sounds good?"

She nodded. "Sounds reasonable to me."

"Should we have any rules?" I asked.

"I prefer conversations to rules," Mark said.

"I like that," I said.

"I think it's important for us all to check in with each other," Narisha said. "It's helpful that Mark and I are already friends, but I think polycule meetings would be good. We could do them here or pick a public spot. Whatever works for everyone."

"How often would we do these meetings?" Mark asked. "I know you two can probably process day in and day out, but I have less emotional needs."

"Once a month?" Narisha suggested.

Mark shrugged. "All right."

"So, our relationships are entirely separate. We all agreed?" Narisha asked.

"Yep," I said.

"Yes, ma'am," Mark replied.

"Good." Narisha smiled. "I think we've covered a lot of territory today. What do you both think?"

"I think we did good," I said.

"I assume Narisha is here for the rest of the day?" Mark asked.

"I intended to stay until tomorrow," Narisha said. "If you want her after that, she's all yours."

He chuckled and sat back. "All right, all right. I know when it's time for me to go."

"Thank you for coming over today, even though it was just to chat," I said.

"Of course." He stood. "It was important to you. I had to come."

Gratitude spread across my face. "I'm glad to have you around."

"Don't I know it," he said with a smile.

"I'll see you tomorrow."

"Until then," he said. He turned to Narisha and waved. "Take good care of her now, won't you?"

"Don't worry, she's in good hands," Narisha said confidently.

The sun shone brightly through the opened windows. I felt like we had done it. We had beaten back the shadows that oppressed us, the spectres of jealousy, and we were really doing it. We were going to be living a polyamorous lifestyle, and everyone was on board. I couldn't be happier.

The next day, I drove to Mark's place. He was busy during the day, so I headed over just before rush hour. It was my favourite time of day. The sun was sitting low in the sky, the clouds bursting with orange and pink colours. It was a calm time. A time I often took for reflection, especially with my hands on the wheel.

So much had happened, and I was still somewhat overwhelmed when I thought about it. But accompanying that was a strong feeling of contentment. I had my chosen family all together. I had dealt with my ex. Mark and I were on the same page, and we were going to work together with Narisha to keep our poly group working smoothly.

It was hard to imagine life as a monogamous person now. Being attached to two people would fulfill so many of my needs. I had never thought about how much I missed men when I was with women and how much I missed women when I was with men. Now, I had the option to date both, and I had their blessing.

I knew there were difficulties ahead. I hadn't experienced any intense jealousy yet, but I knew it would probably manifest at some point, maybe once Narisha started dating or when Mark felt romantic feelings for someone else. But they would help me through it. I wouldn't be alone in this. And I appreciated that more than anything.

I turned on some music, delighting in the nostalgic sounds. Things that made me feel something. I was in love with falling in love, and now I had the opportunity to love more than one person. I could experience the high of being affectionate with more than one person at a time. But the best part about all of this was that I didn't have to stay stuck in my familiar cycle of falling in love, attaching myself to one person, and feeling alone. I had created links with multiple people, and they would be there for me.

I never knew it was possible to love more than one person this way, openly and ethically. I had loved many people but at different times. Now, I could love as much as I wanted. Right now, I was satisfied with what I had. But I was open to the possibilities. For the moment, I was ready to enjoy the company and comfort of my partners. I didn't need any more drama.

I pulled into Mark's driveway. He was waiting outside for me. As I emerged from my car, he opened his arms up wide. I fell into his embrace.

"I'm glad you're here," he said.

"And I'm not going anywhere," I replied.

He rested his chin on my head. "Even if things get complicated?"

"Even then," I said. "Let them get as complicated as they want. I have you and Narisha with me. We'll weather the storm."

We held hands and entered his apartment. As new as I was to polyamory, I knew that no matter what problems we encountered, we'd be able to solve them together. Besides, life would be boring without some complications, wouldn't it?

About the Author

Niamh Norwood is a self-proclaimed geek with a constellation of interests. She obtained her M.A. in English Literature from Carleton University in 2017. She has published short fiction, poetry, novels, and comics. In her free time, she can be found playing the harp, doing "karate as well as Rob McElhenney", and crying over Supercorp being (not) canon.

Acknowledgements

This book is a love letter to my lovers and almost-lovers, and so I need to thank them first and foremost. I want to thank my Muse for inspiring me to keep creating.

Thank you to the Renaissance team for making this possible!

www.ingramcontent.com/pod-product-compliance
Lightning Source LLC
Chambersburg PA
CBHW060320310726
48976CB00007B/2393